"I'm not drunk," Carter said. "Only bold."

"Bold?" Tori swallowed, half afraid she was tempting fate by asking, and half afraid that she wasn't.

"Bold enough to do this." His arm slipped around her waist, and he pulled her close. The loofah ended up pressed tight between them, and he shifted against it, his chuckle soft against her ear. "Hang on to that, sweetheart. Maybe later we can find an interesting use for it."

"I can think of a few," she said. Tori heard her own voice, soft and sultry, and the sound pulled her back to reality. Closing her eyes, she backed away. "I—I'm sorry. I can't do this. I want to, but I can't."

He pulled his T-shirt over his head. "Yes, babe, you can." He dropped the shirt, now soaked, to the floor of the tub. "Sex camp, remember? Intimacy. Young lovers with an amazing sex life looking to spice it up."

"I think I already proved that we can fake it just fine."

He unbuttoned his shorts, then started to tug at the zipper. "Is that what you do? Fake it?"

She bit back a smile, determined not to give in. "I've faked it once or twice."

The shorts came off, dropping into the tub with a wet splat. "Not with me you haven't...."

Dear Reader,

A strong-willed, sexy man. An equally strong-willed woman with a chip on her shoulder. Both with a history. And both with guns...

When FBI agents Tori and Carter introduced themselves to me, the combination was just too intriguing to ignore. Tori is a woman who goes after what she wants. And what she wants is a prime assignment with the FBI. Carter wants the same thing. But when they're forced to spend time—some very intimate time—together at a sex resort to investigate a blackmail scheme, both begin to question their own desires.

I hope you enjoy Tori and Carter's story. I wrote it during the months surrounding the tragedy of September 11, and this reader letter is more than just an introduction to the story. It's also a thank-you for all the mail I received from readers telling me how much reading a romance and escaping for a few hours meant to you. Your e-mail and letters couldn't have been more appreciated.

Happy reading,

Julie Kenner

P.S. Keep those letters coming! You can write to me at P.O. Box 151417, Austin, TX 78715-1417, or e-mail me at julie@juliekenner.com.

Books by Julie Kenner

HARLEQUIN TEMPTATION
772—NOBODY DOES IT BETTER
801—RECKLESS
840—INTIMATE FANTASY

HARLEQUIN BLAZE
16—L.A. CONFIDENTIAL

UNDERCOVER LOVERS
Julie Kenner

HARLEQUIN®

TORONTO • NEW YORK • LONDON
AMSTERDAM • PARIS • SYDNEY • HAMBURG
STOCKHOLM • ATHENS • TOKYO • MILAN • MADRID
PRAGUE • WARSAW • BUDAPEST • AUCKLAND

To Richard and Shelley. Congrats!
And thanks for "buying every one of them."
Love you guys!

ISBN 0-373-25993-X

UNDERCOVER LOVERS

Copyright © 2002 by Julia Beck Kenner.

Visit us at www.eHarlequin.com

Printed in U.S.A.

1

CARTER SINCLAIR shifted in the leather chair and pushed his shoulder-length hair out of his face. Damn, but he longed for a haircut and a shower. For three harrowing years he'd been knee-deep in murderous, sleazebag scum, and he was nearing the end of his rope. Just hours ago, he'd been pulled off of his current undercover gig, and he could only hope the reason was the change of assignment he'd put in for.

Across from him, Assistant Director Evan Kincaid put down the phone, then flipped open a manila file folder on his desk. Carter recognized his personnel file. Hell, he'd seen it enough recently.

Kincaid peered at him over the rims of his half glasses, a portrait of the President and the FBI seal on the wall behind him. "I understand you're looking for a new assignment."

"Yes, sir. I'd like a permanent assignment to a field office. I'm hoping to go in as the special agent in charge."

"Why?"

"It's all there in my file, sir."

Kincaid leaned back, crossing his arms over his chest. "Humor me."

Carter suppressed a snort. He'd been through a whole battery of psych exams, and still he had to prove himself. "I'm looking for a change in lifestyle, sir.

Chasing drug dealers doesn't hold the appeal it once did."

"Understandable. You've been deep undercover for a long time."

Carter sat up a little straighter as Kincaid continued to flip through his file. After four requests for a transfer, that wasn't the response he'd been expecting. When he'd left the Waxahachie, Texas, police department to join the Bureau, he'd longed for the chance to hunt down the criminals that preyed on ordinary folks. He'd gotten the chance, and he'd helped put away more hardened criminals than he had fingers and toes to count.

But now Carter was just plain tired. Emotionally, physically. Hell, he was so tired his fingernails ached. He either needed a new assignment or a new job. But Carter loved the Bureau, and that's why he'd spent the last two months trying to push through this request.

He cleared his throat, and Kincaid looked up from the folder. "Does that mean the Bureau's going to facilitate my request?" Carter asked.

Kincaid pushed back from his desk. "That depends on you."

"Sir?"

"Have you been following the news? Celebrity blackmail?"

Carter nodded, not sure where this was going. "I've heard a bit about it. Some big-shot Hollywood director. A Wall Street tycoon. And a Congressman, I think."

In truth, he'd have to have been on Mars to have missed the news. Some scumbag was selling sexual secrets. Reputations were being ruined, deals destroyed, and key political players were suddenly bending to the will of unseen blackmailers.

"They're just the tip of the iceberg," Kincaid said. "The high-profile victims. The ones who are willing to go public instead of succumbing to the perp who's trying to put the pressure on. And," Kincaid continued, "that's why the FBI's getting involved."

"A case?" Carter asked, sitting up even straighter.

Kincaid nodded, then grabbed the top folder off of his in box. He pulled out a thick report and rifled through the pages. "Our information suggests that there are quite a few more victims out there—ordinary folks with a lot to lose who haven't contacted us or their local police yet." Kincaid put the report in the folder and slid the whole thing across the desk toward Carter.

That made sense. Carter reached for the folder and skimmed the summary stapled to the full report. Some agent holed up in a cubicle somewhere had done an excellent job of tracking down loose ends. The author had discovered a link between all the known victims— sometime within the last two years, all the victims had visited a resort just north of Santa Barbara, California. A rather interesting resort, from the looks of it. Called the Kama Resort, the place was run by a sex therapist with a call-in radio show that Carter had heard once or twice.

"It's a sex camp," he said, setting the file on the desk.

"More or less, yes." Kincaid reached for the folder and returned it to its proper stack. "According to the brochure, it caters to couples who are hoping to..." He broke off, looking slightly uncomfortable as his hand twisted in the air in search of the proper word. "...to improve their, uh, *intimacy.*"

Amused, Carter kicked back, stretching his long legs

out until the toes of his loafers grazed the polished wood. "Like I said, a sex camp."

"Yes, well, there you have it."

"Does the Bureau suspect the owner?"

"Interesting question. We checked him out, and he seems clean." Kincaid leaned back in his chair. "But at this point we just don't know. It could be him, a staff member, a frequent guest. Hell, there might be no connection to the resort at all. The background of the extortion victims could just be a coincidence."

"So what does this have to do with me?" Carter asked.

"The FBI's been asked to participate in a task force. We're working with the sheriff's department in Santa Barbara County along with the local police department. The task force is sending in a team to investigate the resort," Kincaid said. "Like I said, it might be coincidence, but I'm not a big believer in coincidence myself."

"And I'm on the task force."

"Not only are you on the task force, agent, you're heading it up and leading the undercover team. Unless you have something else planned."

Carter swallowed a grimace. Hell, yes, he had something else planned. A nice desk job in one of the FBI's many bureaus. Maybe even back home in Texas. The last thing he wanted was to jump from one undercover job to another. He wanted out of that grind, and if Kincaid wasn't willing to cut him loose, then maybe it really was time to turn in his resignation.

"Sinclair?"

Carter sat up. "Sir, I'm afraid this isn't an assignment I can accept. I'm not interested in—"

"Working undercover. I know."

"Yes, sir."

"Well, maybe I can persuade you."

"No, sir. I'm not—"

"If you do a good job, I can guarantee you a new assignment. A field office, if that's what you want. Your pick of location." He spread his hands wide. "Carte blanche. But only if..." He trailed off.

"I know, I know."

"Well? Think you can handle one more undercover job? After all, it's not like you'll be up to your elbows in crack addicts. Considering your background, this will be more like a vacation."

Carter wasn't sure about that, but he knew enough to recognize when he was beat. He might not want to go undercover again, but if he aced this assignment, at least it would be the last time. Resigned, he exhaled. "Who's on my team?"

"You and the author of the report. You're both scheduled to fly into Burbank, pick up a rental car and your papers from the local field office and then drive up the coast to the resort."

"That's it? One person? I thought you said a team, not a partner."

Kincaid leaned back again, his chair squeaking. "Like you said, it's a sex camp. You'll have task force support on the outside, but you and a female agent will go in alone. You and Agent Lowell will—"

"Lowell?" Carter leaned forward. Surely, he'd heard wrong. "Not Tori Lowell?"

Kincaid gave him that above-the-rim glance. "You know her?"

A complicated question. For Carter, Tori Lowell had always meant trouble—of both the good and bad kind.

Carter decided to brush it off. "We went to the academy together."

"Then you may or may not realize that she's been desk jockeying since Quantico. And damn good at it, too. But she's also been itching for an undercover assignment, and since she discovered this link, we've decided to grant her request." Again, he aimed that assessing glance over his glasses. "If you know Lowell, then I'm sure you know her reputation."

"Yes, sir," Carter mumbled.

"Good. Because I'm trusting you to keep her in line. The woman's a good agent, but she's a loose cannon, and since this is her first time undercover, I don't want her playing Rambo."

Irritation welled in Carter's gut. "So I'm babysitting?"

Kincaid shook his head. "No. You're just leading your team. You do your job well, and we'll have no problem pushing through your request for reassignment."

Carter's hands tightened on the armrests. Kincaid could call it what he wanted, but it sounded damn close to baby-sitting to him. Either that, or blackmail. Keep the overeager agent in line and get a new assignment; fail and get sent back to undercover hell.

Not exactly his dream job.

Kincaid leaned back, looking Carter straight in the eye. "I trust this isn't a problem?"

For half a second, Carter considered telling Kincaid to find another sucker. Then common sense caught up to him. "No, sir." This assignment was his ticket out of his current placement, and for that, he'd put up with a lot. Even Tori Lowell.

It was only when he'd stepped out of Kincaid's office, the full brief clasped in his hand, that he realized the extent of what he'd agreed to—he and Tori posing as husband and wife at a sex camp. *A sex camp.*

Sighing, he headed down the hall toward the elevator. He needed to get out of the building before he did something stupid like walk into Kincaid's office, throw the file on his desk and tell him to find some other agent to lead the team.

But no, there were a hundred reasons for him to take this assignment, and only one reason to walk away.

And surely that reason had changed over the last three years. Despite what Kincaid said, she couldn't still be the same ultra-competitive, smart-mouthed, sexy-as-hell woman he'd sparred with at Quantico, could she?

As a man, Carter had been attracted to her from the first day they were assigned to the same class. Tori was brilliant and ambitious, and her academy achievements had pushed Carter. He owed his success at the academy to their pervasive competition.

But while she might have all the makings of a smart and intuitive agent, she'd also been a wild card, and if Kincaid was right, she still was. The daughter of a highly celebrated undercover agent, Tori had made no secret of the fact that she intended to follow in her father's footsteps and that she'd do anything to get there.

Dating while at Quantico was discouraged by the powers that be, but not forbidden, and Carter had been entranced enough to go against protocol. Almost daily, Carter had asked Tori out for coffee or to grab a pizza and some beer at the Boardroom, the bar located above the cafeteria at Quantico. She'd repeatedly turned him down cold. Repeatedly, that is, until the week before graduation. When he'd asked her then, she'd accepted.

Carter blew out a breath, his body tightening as he remembered the way she'd looked that night. She'd worn a black dress and, though he'd seen her in jogging shorts, there was just something about a woman in stockings and heels. He'd taken her into Alexandria for dancing, and they'd worked up quite a sweat, each trying to go a little bit longer, a little bit harder, than the other. They'd cooled off afterward with vodka tonics. Not that Carter had really cooled off. Just the opposite, in fact. Simply being near Tori seemed to ignite his blood to near boiling.

Apparently Tori had heated up a bit, too. Because by the time they reached the dorms, neither one could keep their hands off the other. God, he'd been desperate for her, and he'd pinned her in the circle of his arms right under the stairway leading to her room.

She hadn't protested, either. Her arms had slipped around his neck, and her lips... He sighed with the memory. Oh, the taste of her lips.

He'd moved closer, breaking the circle of his arms so he could touch her, stroke her body under that slinky, sexy dress. She'd moaned, her breath soft and hot against his ear. He remembered his head spinning, not only from the alcohol, but from the knowledge that this woman—this woman he'd been competing with during their entire tenure at Quantico—actually wanted him as much as he wanted her.

His mouth had explored hers, his hands stroking her silky soft shoulder, then down lower to trace the curve of her breast. She'd moaned, and the sound had acted on him with as much force as if she'd dropped to her knees and taken him in her mouth. He'd pulled her closer, wanting more, wanting *everything*, and knowing they should go inside one of their rooms but unwilling to do anything that would take her out of his embrace.

She'd leaned back, and their eyes met. At first, her mouth had curved into a smile, but then she'd frowned. Her eyes had widened, and she'd jerked backward. "I have to go," she said.

She might as well have slapped him. Carter had been too stunned to move. "What?" he asked. "What is it?"

With increasing urgency, she'd pressed against his arm. "I have to *go*."

She broke free and ran down the hall, then up the stairs, her footsteps echoing through the corridor. He turned, instinctively looking around to see if anyone had witnessed her odd behavior. Nobody. The halls were completely empty.

It was only after the echo died that he realized what must have happened. It had all been a ruse. Their final tests were coming up, and so far he'd managed to pull ahead of her in every area. The Bureau didn't formally rank its graduates, but everyone still knew who had the top spot. Right then, it was Carter. But Tori wanted that spot. Wanted it bad. And, damn it, apparently she even wanted it enough to try a little seduction to throw him off his game. He didn't know why she'd run. Maybe she'd chickened out. Or maybe that was her game plan all along—get him hot and then get out of there.

He sighed. A damn shame. For a moment there, he'd thought they'd actually connected. He should have known better. Tori was too competitive by half. If anyone ever connected with her, it would be a damn miracle. He'd only wished she had run out on him before he'd got a major hard-on. Because all he'd had to look forward to that evening was a long, cold shower.

At the elevator, Carter sighed as he pulled himself out of his memories. He'd been her nemesis back then, and knowing Tori, she still had it in for him. At the very least, Tori was going to be less than enthusiastic about partnering with the man who—at least in her mind—stole her number one ranking in firearms, physical training and the classroom portion of their academy training.

He stepped onto the elevator, his mind reeling. Not that he was still interested in Tori. He got enough excitement in his job. She might have once been roll-in-the-sheets material, but nowadays, Carter's interest in women leaned toward the more stable variety.

Swallowing a snort, he shook his head at his foolishness. No matter how he felt about her now, the truth was, he'd spent his days and nights at Quantico with a permanent hard-on, courtesy of a woman who drove him completely nuts and who probably never wanted to see him again.

A woman who was now his partner. A woman he was supposed to keep out of trouble.

The elevator doors slid shut, and he pressed his forehead against the cool metal.

Damn. What the hell had he gotten himself into?

"EAGLE'S NEST, this is Redbird. I'm in place." Special Agent Tori Lowell ducked behind the Dumpster in downtown Hogan's Alley, ignoring the repulsive odor of rotting food and who knows what else and waited for Murphy's reply to register in her earpiece. She didn't have long to wait.

"Roger, Redbird." A burst of static, then, "Hatchlings, the rest of you give me an update."

"Bluebird here. In place. No action."

"Sparrow. Same here."

"Seagull. Someone's coming. Hang tight."

Tori monitored the conversation through her earpiece, adrenaline pumping through her veins. The area behind the Dumpster stank to high heaven, and she longed to get out and see what was going on. But her orders had been firm—on this routine training mission, she wasn't to do anything but observe unless she was given a direct order.

She sighed, resting her forehead against the rusty metal. How the devil was she ever supposed to prove herself if her superiors never gave her the opportunity? Carter Sinclair had been working in the field since they left the academy. Apparently, *his* career hadn't suffered from their little liaison that night at Quantico.

She tightened her hand around the barrel of her gun, struggling to control her temper. She was just as good an agent as Carter—maybe even better—and yet she'd been locked inside an office building. Her superiors told her it was because she was good at research, and her mentor in the Bureau—an overprotective family friend—backed up that assessment.

But Tori didn't believe it. She was too good to be chained to a desk. Which meant the only explanation was Carter. She'd made a mistake and had agreed to go out with the super-sexy agent. And then, when the wine and the moonlight had gotten the better of them, she'd succumbed to heaven in his arms.

She sighed at the memory. Oh, God, it *had* been heaven. At least until they'd been seen. She'd never discovered who their witness was, but she'd seen him in the shadows, watching her and Carter. He must have reported them; there was no other explanation. Her little tryst with Carter was reported to the higher-

ups, and Carter, being a guy, still landed the primo assignments. Tori, however, got stuck in FBI hell.

It wasn't fair; it wasn't fair at all.

Bang! Crack!

Shots fired. Tori pressed her back against the brick
wall, one hand on a pile of empty paint cans for balance. Her whole body tingled as she fought the urge to
leap out and see what was going on.

Stay put, stay put, stay put. She repeated the mantra in
her head, hoping the order to engage would squawk in
her earpiece. More than anything, she wanted to get off
the research and analysis grind. Technically, she was a
field agent, but it was a rare day when she actually got
to go out in the field. No, one little mistake, and she'd
been stuck pushing paper in Investigative Services Di-
vision. She was good at the research, good at the analysis, but, damn it, she hadn't joined the FBI to sit at a
desk.

Her father had been an amazing undercover operative. Legendary, even. True, he'd hardly ever been
around, but that was only because his work had been
so important. When he'd died, Tori and her mom had
just about died, too. From that moment on, Tori had
wanted to fill her dad's shoes.

She hoped she had what it took, but she really didn't
know. Tori had always been good in the classroom, but
the real world was untested and, frankly, that made
her nervous as hell. She'd always been among the best,
but what if she wasn't any more? The thought was so-
bering. She needed to prove herself, to live up to her father's standards. And she'd do whatever she had to.

But so much was working against her. She was a
woman in a man's world. True, there were more female agents in the Bureau than ever before, but that

didn't mean the women didn't have to work harder to get to the same place.

Her every attempt to get an undercover assignment had been foiled, and she'd spent the duration of her FBI career with her butt in a chair and her eyes on a computer monitor. The work was interesting, no doubt about that, but it wasn't the same as going undercover. So far, her efforts had hit a brick wall, and she was angry at herself for helping to put that wall in place. She'd been attracted to Carter from the day they'd met. And, considering the many times he'd asked her out, that attraction was reciprocated.

She'd given in against her better judgment, and she'd been paying the price for years.

Now, though, she had a real chance. Follow orders, do the job and—hopefully—get the transfer. She held her breath, waiting for the order to engage.

Unfortunately, her earpiece remained stubbornly silent.

The alleyway, however, wasn't nearly as quiet. Pounding footsteps broke the stillness. Someone running. And a voice shouting for him to halt and put his hands up.

Closer…*closer*…

She could apprehend him. She was in position. She could do it. All she needed was the go-ahead.

But still nothing in her headphone. *Damn.*

"Eagle's Nest, this is Redbird. I've got a bead on the perp. Do I have the go-ahead?"

A burst of static hit her ear. "Negative, Redbird."

She opened her mouth to argue, then closed it, her body thrumming like a live wire from the pent-up energy.

Instinct and training told her to go ahead and do her

job. Common sense told her to follow orders and sit tight.

The perp pulled closer, near enough that she could hear his breathing. Damn Murphy! There wasn't any reason she shouldn't get this guy.

She heard him right there on the other side of the Dumpster. Her hand closed around butt of her gun. *Stay put, stay put.*

In an instant, she changed her mind, reaching for one of the empty paint cans. Her field of vision was limited, but she pulled her arm back, and when he passed, she heaved, hitting him square between the shoulders and knocking him to the ground. "Hands behind your head," she yelled as she pulled her gun, still staying behind the Dumpster.

On the ground, the perp groaned and locked his fingers at his neck. Mentally, Tori patted herself on the back. She'd got him. And she hadn't disobeyed orders. Not technically, anyway.

Special Agent Travis Murphy, his hands shoved into the pockets of his FBI parka, lumbered toward them, then bent at the side of the perp. "You okay, son?" Considering Murphy wasn't treating the guy as a hardened criminal, Tori assumed the training exercise was over.

The guy sat up, rubbing his back. "Fine, sir."

Murphy nodded, then patted him on the shoulder. "Go get yourself checked out. She got you pretty hard."

The perp—an agent Tori didn't recognize—shot her a decidedly dirty look. "Yeah, she did."

She shrugged, trying to look innocent and vindicated. Her eyes met Murphy's. "I got the perp. Sir."

"You disobeyed a direct order."

"No, sir. I stayed behind the Dumpster and I—"

"Damn it, Lowell, don't split hairs with me. That's not a game you want to be playing."

She sucked in a breath, biting back her automatic retort about the whole point of training ops being to train agents to take action, not sit back like meek little bunnies. But she knew what his response would be—Hogan's Alley was a fake town set up just for this kind of thing. The FBI had strict rules about the scenarios that went down there. Yada, yada, et cetera and so forth.

She pulled her thoughts to the present, where Murphy was still chewing her out.

"How the hell am I supposed to evaluate your fitness for the field if you can't even follow a simple instruction? Not to mention that you probably dislocated O'Henry's shoulder." He sighed, his ruddy face coloring even more than usual in the summer heat.

Tori licked her lips, the truth fighting with her pride. On the pride side, she knew—she just *knew*—she'd done the right thing, made the right call. If she hadn't thrown that can, the perp would have gotten away. The robbery would have gone down, and the FBI would have no one in custody.

On the truth side, Tori knew she'd disobeyed a direct order. In her mind, though, so long as none of the good guys got hurt, following orders wasn't anywhere near as important as catching the bad guys. Too bad no one had asked for her opinion.

"I'm sorry, sir. It was an instinct, sir."

"Bullshit. Quit trying to be your father, Lowell." He bent his head to look at her over the rim of his glasses. "This is going in your file. I'm sorry, but I don't have any choice."

Tori's heart sank even as her ire bloomed. She managed to catch his sleeve before he turned away. "Travis!"

The frown he shot her was anything but amused.

"I mean, Agent Murphy." She lowered her voice. "Give me a break here. I've been pushing a computer since I joined the Bureau. I want to get out in the field. I want an undercover assignment."

"Then do the job you're assigned and earn it."

"Earn it? I earned it at Quantico!"

He glared.

Tori squared her shoulders. "What about the report I turned in last week? Those blackmail incidents." She started counting on her fingers. "The senator, that real estate developer and even that movie director. There's a connection there. Did you read the report? And those are only the ones we know about. Someone's running a scam out there. If I could only get out to—"

"Damn it, Tori. Your job is analysis, and you do a damn good job of it."

The words came out harsh, but after a few moments, the older man's face softened, and she recognized the familiar features she knew so well. Travis Murphy and Tori's dad had been best friends at the academy and had worked closely together after that. When Mark Lowell had died, Uncle Travis had stepped in, watching out for Tori and her mother.

Now, she had to wonder if he was regretting being as good a role model as he'd been. Maybe if Travis hadn't doted on her so much, she wouldn't have followed in his and her father's footsteps. After all, it wasn't too late to take that accounting job at one of the Big Eight firms.

She stifled an unladylike snort. Not damn likely.

"I may be good at it, sir, but I didn't sign up to work

a desk. I have a degree in accounting, remember? I walked away from the desk job option. I joined the Bureau—"

"To be an undercover agent. Like your dad." His eyes were sad, remembering. "I know. And I suppose I can't protect you forever. But you're not going to make it to the top by bending the rules."

Her dad had bent plenty of rules, but Tori knew when to keep her mouth shut. Instead, she closed her eyes and counted to ten. It was only while she was counting that Murphy's words sunk in. Slowly, she opened her eyes, hoping she wasn't setting herself up for more disappointment. "What do you mean, you can't protect me forever?" She drew in a breath. "Am I getting an undercover assignment?"

The thin line of Murphy's mouth remained firm, but he nodded. "Yeah, kid. It looks like you are."

Tori's breath caught in her throat. "What? When? With who?" Her words tripped off her tongue, and it was all she could do not to shake Murphy and have him spill the entire story right then.

He held up a hand, laughing. "Hold on. You're scheduled for a full briefing in about an hour. Right now, all I know is that you're investigating the allegations in your report. And you'll be working with one of the guys from your class at the Academy."

"Doug Leyman?" she offered, suggesting one of her study buddies.

"Carter something," Murphy said. Tori's stomach twisted even as she wondered why Carter's name would be unfamiliar to Murphy. Considering how much it had affected her career, surely her little tryst with Carter was legendary within the Bureau by now.

But Murphy looked genuinely clueless. "Carter Simmons, maybe?" he said.

"Sinclair," Tori corrected. For years, she'd lived with the Carter mistake hanging around her neck like an albatross, and now this? She looked Murphy in the eye, wondering if the universe wasn't playing some cruel joke on her. But he didn't look to be joking, and she exhaled, standing up straighter and meeting his eye. "The agent's name is Carter Sinclair."

2

TORI SAT ON A BENCH outside the Burbank airport and read through her report on the Kama Resort for the umpteenth time, going over every nuance that had led to her putting together the connection between the blackmail victims, and to her conclusion that there were more victims out there still unaccounted for.

Her eyes drifted over the page, taking in every word. Not that she actually needed to read it. Heck, at this point she could practically recite the thing from memory. But reading kept her mind off Carter, and that had to be a good thing.

Carter. She shouldn't have let her thoughts go there, because now she was stuck thinking about him. And she didn't want to think about him. Thinking about him only made her frustrated and angry and a whole host of other emotions she had no business entertaining. And to find out she was going to be working in close quarters with him—and at a *sex resort*, no less.

She shivered, not sure if it was a blessing or a curse.

She recalled his face—that cocky grin, those brooding eyes. And lashes so long they'd be feminine on any man other than Carter.

A curse. Definitely a curse. And not only because he frustrated her on so many levels. Sure, he'd been her nemesis throughout their tenure at the academy, and sure, he'd gotten the prime assignments while she'd been pounding a keyboard. But she was a big girl. She knew Carter hadn't been the one holding her back. No, that dubious honor belonged to her superiors. And while she was pissed as hell, she wasn't pissed at Carter. Well, not much, anyway.

But this was *her* case. She'd put the pieces together. She'd spent hours getting blisters on her butt while she made phone call after phone call tracking down leads that tied the players to the resort. She'd been the one who'd burned up the Internet trying to find missing pieces of information. And she was the one who'd drafted the report that got the ball rolling.

By all rights, she should be leading the team. But was she? Nope. Once again, Carter had bested her, and she was reporting to him.

The situation stank.

Not that she'd really expected anything else. After all, she'd been stuck in a closet with a computer for the last few years while Carter had been out doing the job she deserved. Not that anyone had ever come out and said anything about her indiscretion with Carter. Instead, her superiors had consistently praised her brains even while citing her past insubordination. Okay, so maybe she didn't always follow protocol, but lots of agents didn't, right? The point was to win in the end.

No, Tori was certain that her fate was a product of her impetuous encounter with Carter. Hopefully this new mission meant she'd finally paid her dues and was getting an assignment based on merit.

Of course, it wasn't as if they'd given her the type of assignment she'd been wanting. She'd hoped to infiltrate a drug ring or buddy up with members of the mob. Instead, she was getting undercover light—pretending to be married at a sex resort. Not what she'd expected, but beggars couldn't be choosers.

And even though she was stuck as the underling, she intended to do everything in her power to shine on this job. And if that meant impressing—and obeying—Carter Sinclair, well, she could handle that.

She'd try anyway. She intended to work her tush off in the process. Because when this was all over, she wanted to be out in the field permanently. And if Carter was her stepping-stone, then so be it. She was ten times the agent he was, and in the end, she'd surely prove it—even while being the subservient little underling.

As it was, she'd already outlined a number of ways they could get the case rolling. Her eyes skimmed over the neatly printed list, only one of many papers in her portfolio. She'd worked on her plan over the course of the entire flight from Washington to California and she had some great ideas for jump-starting their research and investigating the potential perps.

Carter was sure to be impressed.

"Looks like the gang's all here."

Tori flinched at the achingly familiar voice behind her. A voice that forced her to admit that, on a certain forbidden level, she was excited about seeing him again. *Damn.*

Gathering herself, she shifted on the bench to face him. She drew in a quick breath, hoping he didn't notice. Carter had always been good-looking, but she hadn't expected the commanding presence she was facing. Somehow, he'd matured since she'd seen him last, and the change suited him.

"Solved the case yet, Lowell?" he asked.

She smiled, the same cool and collected smile she'd

used a hundred times to ward off unwelcome advances. "Not just yet, Sinclair. But I've got a self-imposed deadline. By noon tomorrow, I'll have this thing whipped."

"Noon?" His head cocked slightly as he looked her in the eye. "You're slipping, Lowell. I plan to have this case wrapped up by ten at the latest."

She set her jaw. "Dawn, then. I'll smoke out our bad guy by dawn." She looked him in the eye. "No matter what, I'll solve it before you do."

His mouth twitched, but he didn't throw another challenge at her. *Good.* Chalk one up for her side.

With a quick flick, she snapped her portfolio closed, then stood up, her hand out in a formal greeting. "I've been working on our plan of attack. I thought we could start at the local paper. I've already called their morgue and asked them to pull any articles about the resort so we—"

"Good to see you, too, Tori." He started walking past her toward the baggage claim area, ignoring her hand and her comments.

Okay. That was *not* what she had in mind. Gathering her bags, she hurried after him. "Carter?" No response.

Damn it, he was ignoring her on purpose, and she really wasn't in the mood for that kind of power play.

Determination renewed, she shifted her duffel's strap on her shoulder and upped her speed, catching up to him as he eased onto the down escalator. She squeezed onto the same step, forcing him toward the handrail, his body close enough that she caught a subtle hint of his aftershave. "We're not going to get anywhere if you ignore me," she said.

He turned, leaning against the rail and ignoring the

signs imploring him to Please Hold Handrail. For a second he just stood there, looking at her, his eyes dark and dangerous. "We're not going to get anywhere," he said, throwing back her words, "if you start working this case on your own without talking to me or the rest of the task force first."

"Working this—?"

"Calling the newspaper office? What were you thinking? Word could get back to whoever's running this scam that someone's poking around. We're supposed to be undercover, remember? And that means not jumping in wearing bright orange neon."

Her fingernails dug into her palm as she tried to control her flaring temper. "I'm not an idiot, Sinclair. I said I was a reporter for a travel magazine doing some background research on California resorts. Nothing suspicious. Nothing that's going to jeopardize your precious first time leading a mission."

She crossed her arms over her chest and waited for him to apologize, but he said nothing. Well, fine. Wasn't *this* going to be a pleasant assignment?

As they stepped off the escalator, she matched him stride for stride, her irritation growing with each step. "Do you want to hear my other ideas? Or are you going to just keep on ignoring me?" Probably he expected her to simply do whatever he said without question and not even participate. Hell, this was *their* mission, even if he was technically in charge. And Tori intended to see to it that she was a full participant, no matter what Carter might have planned.

This time he stopped, and she gave herself two mental points. "Look, Tori. I'm tired. I haven't slept in three days." He shifted his carry-on to the opposite shoulder, then smiled at her. A real smile, not the least bit condescending. Damn him, how the hell was she supposed to stay righteously indignant if he was going to make nice?

"I'm not ignoring you," he added. "I just want to get my luggage, get our car and then get on the road. Once we're on the highway, you can talk all you want." He fumbled in his pocket and pulled out his baggage claim ticket. "Deal?"

She wanted to argue. Hell, she even opened her mouth and started to. But the facts were the facts, and as much as she hated it, Carter was in charge. Not only that, but he was being civil—at least a little—and that was something she hadn't really expected considering their history and how they'd started out a few minutes ago.

She couldn't say her anger melted, but it was definitely getting soft around the edges. And hadn't her grandmother always said she'd catch more flies with honey? Tori had always hated that saying, but at the moment it seemed uniquely appropriate.

He stood still, waiting for her answer, his arms crossed as a flood of passengers maneuvered around them.

Her instincts told her to fight. To make him understand—right then, right there—that she wasn't just some second-fiddle partner. She wanted to be part of the decision-making process, and she didn't intend to let him overshadow her. But something in his eyes stalled her resolve, and she caved.

"Fine," she said, hoping against hope that she wasn't somehow handing Carter the upper hand for the entire length of their assignment. She lifted her chin. "We'll talk in the car."

CARTER EXHALED in relief. He'd expected a fight. Hell, where Tori was concerned, he *always* expected a fight. And he had to wonder what had caused her to back off.

Still, he didn't intend to wonder for too long. Right then, he'd take whatever little gifts she handed him. And he fully anticipated that they'd be sparring like old times once they reached the car.

Right now, though, he needed some time alone. He'd known for days they'd be working together, but it wasn't until he saw her sitting in the lobby, her shoulder-length brown curls hanging loose as she hunched over a pad of yellow paper, that reality had conked him on the head. He'd seen her sitting there, and all the old feelings had come rushing back—competitiveness, frustration and, yes, desire.

The frustration made sense. After all, she had a reputation for shooting from the hip, and Carter liked to follow the rules. He'd also expected the competitiveness; they'd been neck-and-neck at the academy, and he'd had no reason to expect that either of them would be completely able to keep the past in the past.

The desire, though... Well, that's what floored him. At the academy, he'd wanted her. No question about it. But she'd only been using him, and, although she'd left him frustrated as hell that night, it wasn't as if the love of his life had run out on him. No, that bit of lust had been nothing more than hormones. He'd been young and horny, and the fact that she challenged him had excited him.

But he'd grown up since then. No longer did Carter want to be a superagent, spending all his time in the field, surrounding himself with the underbelly of society. No, more and more he was realizing he wanted a simpler lifestyle. He didn't want to leave the Bureau, but he did want a home. A family. A wife, a couple of kids. Maybe even a dog.

Undercover work didn't allow for much of a social life, but he'd managed to work in one or two dates in the last few months. And the women he'd gone out with were looking for the same thing he was. They were nice women. All smart and interesting. And not one packed a pistol.

Exactly the kind of women he wanted.

So why was it that after just a few minutes with Tori his body was reacting like he hadn't gotten laid in a year? Why could he smell her soap even though she was walking a few feet behind him? Why did he have to stifle the urge to turn around and watch the way her breasts moved under that thin cotton T-shirt she wore untucked over her jeans?

Only one answer sprang to mind—that one or two dates over the last few months weren't enough to satisfy the libido of a guy in his early thirties. Too bad for him the hottest woman he'd run into was a woman with a history of driving him nuts. Thank God for self-control.

Unfortunately for him, though, by the time they reached the baggage claim, his self-control was fading, and his body was on hyperdrive. Not that she'd be interested even if he did make a move. Tori had made it more than clear on numerous occasions that she wasn't interested in him, and he sincerely doubted anything had changed in that department.

Besides, even if he thought she'd jump at the chance, he still wouldn't make a move. No matter how hot she was, Carter was a professional. What was between him and Tori was strictly business. And that's all it would ever be.

He turned to her more brusquely than he intended. "Why don't you get the car while I wait for my bag. I'll meet you in front of the rental counter."

"Trying to get rid of me already?" she asked, the corner of her mouth twitching.

He had the absurd desire to kiss her. As if that would somehow show her who was in charge. Or maybe it would show him he wasn't as strong as he thought he was. "Just go," he said, hoping he sounded authoritative and not frustrated that she'd actually nailed his motivation.

Thankfully, she went. He watched her leave, giving in to the urge to enjoy the way she moved in the well-worn jeans and annoyed with himself for letting his self-control slip.

A plethora of black nearly identical bags started going round and round on the conveyor, and he let his mind wander even as he watched for the purple string tied onto the handle that designated his basic black bag.

His instinct in Kincaid's office had been right; he shouldn't have taken this case. No matter what the reward, working with Tori wasn't going to be easy. In fact, it was going to be damn hard. And not just because she was so gung-ho about finally working in the field. He had no idea why she'd been stuck at a desk, but he could smell how badly she wanted a field assignment.

Unfortunately, her overeager attitude had the potential to get them into trouble. He'd had to bite his tongue not to read her the riot act when she'd told him about the stunt she'd pulled at the newspaper morgue. Thankfully, she'd told the story about being a reporter, but still... Didn't she understand that the point was to blend in? They were *undercover* after all. The idea was to get the lay of the land, not to storm in with guns blazing.

But it wasn't her misplaced enthusiasm that was going to make this mission hard. No, the real problem lay in the assignment itself—in the fact that he and Tori Lowell were going undercover together, literally and figuratively.

Too bad for Carter, on this assignment, undercover meant long days and even longer nights with Tori. Pretending to be married, of all things.

And not just any married couple. No, they had to go and pretend to be a married couple looking to spruce up their sex life. He sighed, his entire body tightening at the thought of finally being that intimate with Tori. Not exactly an appropriate reaction from a team leader, and one he intended to nip in the bud.

"Isn't that your bag?"

He started at the sound of her voice so close behind him, then looked in the general direction she was pointing. Sure enough, there was his bag, disappearing into the bowels of the building as it went around on the conveyor. "Damn."

She pressed her lips together, and her blue eyes twinkled. "Lost in thought?" she asked.

"What makes you say that?"

"Because that bag's been around a good three times, and you haven't moved a muscle."

"Just thinking about our game plan," he said, even as he hoped nothing about his voice, stance, manner, *anything*, revealed what he'd been thinking about. "How'd you know it was my bag?" he asked, hoping to change the subject.

"The ribbon." She met his eyes. "You always tied a ribbon on your luggage."

He frowned. They'd traveled together only once before, and he wasn't sure if he was flattered or disturbed that she remembered his habits so well. Fortunately, his luggage reappeared, and he was saved from deciding. He stepped forward and pulled the bag off the belt. "Ready?" he asked.

"You're the boss. If you say I'm ready, then I'm ready."

Carter sighed as he headed toward the exit. Apparently they were back to attitude. "So whatever I say, you're going to do?" He paused long enough to look at her. "If I say jump, you'll jump?"

She rolled one shoulder. "I'm told that's the way this operation's going to go down. You're the big, strong chief, and I'm the subservient underling." Her eyes widened as she peered at him, giving her an innocent quality he knew was total camouflage. "Or have I been misinformed?"

Carter stifled the urge to sigh. He had a feeling he'd be sighing a lot over the next few days, and he didn't want to run through his recommended daily allowance. Instead, he dropped his bag on the ground, turned and faced her, his arms crossed over his chest. "Do we have a problem here, agent?"

She took a step back, her head cocked as if she was surprised by his reaction.

"Well?" He knew he sounded harsh, but he needed to know. There were a hundred reasons working in close proximity to Tori was going to be difficult, and if she intended to go out of her way to make it more so, he wanted to know right off the bat.

For a moment she faced him, that defiant expression

he remembered from the academy flickering across her face. He braced for the worst, but then her expression cleared. "No, *sir*. No problem at all."

"Good. Glad to hear it." They started moving again, and he slipped on his sunglasses as they stepped outside. "So, enlighten me. You said you'd been mapping out a plan. Tell me what you're thinking."

"What?" she asked, her eyes wide with surprise. "The big-shot leader is actually asking the little underling for ideas?"

He almost laughed at her expression, but something told him that her surprise was real, and he kept his face serious. "We're a team, Tori. Which brings to mind the word teamwork. Which implies working together."

She pressed her lips together again, and he sensed hesitation. After a moment, she nodded. "Okay. I've been thinking about lots of things. But the most important is our cover story." Her footsteps quickened to keep pace with his, and he could see her in his peripheral vision. "Mostly, I think we need to get our cover story straight." She paused. "And we'll need some practice."

"Practice?"

"Being a couple. We should practice before checking in to the resort."

Again, his body tightened. The idea of *practicing* with Tori held a certain appeal. Especially for a perfectionist like himself. Hell, they might have to practice for hours and hours....

"—or completely dysfunctional."

He'd missed what she was saying. "Sorry. What was that?"

"I said, we could either be a sexually aware couple looking to add some additional spice to an already pretty perfect relationship, or we could be sexually dysfunctional. You know, unable to get it together and coming to the resort for some much needed help." She paused, as if giving him time to consider all the possibilities. "Which do you think?" her voice was rising with just the hint of challenge.

She'd been baiting him, of course, and now she was expecting a reaction. But he didn't flinch, didn't change his breathing, didn't even look at her. Instead he stared straight ahead and said, "Since it's you and me we're talking about, Agent Lowell, I think we ought to stick with trying new things." He turned then, secure in his composure. "I know your record, agent, and I know me. And I can't imagine either one of us ever failing at anything. And that includes sex."

That got her. Her mouth dropped open, and she stopped cold in the middle of the sidewalk while he continued walking toward the rental car lot. After a second, he heard her laughter, and he allowed himself a simple smile. Two points for the home team, but it was early in the game.

Still, he could say one thing for certain—no matter what else it might be, this assignment wasn't ever going to be dull.

3

THE GUY AT THE CAR RENTAL PLACE told them that the ride from Burbank to Santa Barbara generally took about two hours. As they'd been setting out, Tori had offered to drive, promising Carter she could make it there in one and a half. Like a typical guy, he'd turned down her offer, shifted into first and peeled out.

So she'd spent the last hour and twenty minutes watching him zip up the highway, slowing only to go over hills that might be concealing the local highway patrol.

As they approached the town, Tori crossed her arms over her chest. If she'd offered to make it in *one* hour, Carter probably would have broken the sound barrier.

She turned to him. "So, speed racer, afraid we're going to get there and it'll be gone?" she asked.

He clicked off the Smash Mouth CD he'd been jamming to since they'd left the airport. "Just seeing what she's got," he said, referring to the sleek Jaguar they'd rented. The Kama Resort cost a fortune, and one of the perks of pretending to be a client was that they also got to pretend they had money. Lots and lots of family money.

"Just how long does it take to figure that out?" Tori asked. "You opened her up the second we pulled out of the airport." She'd spent the drive out of the L.A. area getting her notes in order to go over with Carter as soon as they were out of traffic. He'd spent the time popping the clutch, shifting like mad and generally behaving like a guy.

He shrugged, then downshifted as they rounded a curve. "Like all females, cars aren't predictable." He turned to face her, his honey-brown eyes unreadable. "Some take longer to get to know than others."

She laughed. No way was he baiting her that easily. "Like me?" Turning in her seat, she faced him head-on. "Believe me, boss, you're not going to figure me out unless I want to be figured out. And that's a promise."

"You always were cocky." Hooking his finger on the bridge of his glasses, he turned just enough to aim a sideways glance in her direction. "You're also pretty damn inscrutable."

"And you think that's a bad thing?"

"Depends." The car crested a hill, and he paused to glance toward the ocean beating against the beach on their left. "It's good in a woman you're just starting to be interested in." He caught her eye, and the intensity reflected there surprised her. "I mean, there's something exciting—erotic, even—about the unknown. Don't you agree?"

She licked her lips. She'd already decided he wouldn't bait her, but he was sure trying hard enough. And damned if some secret little part of her actually liked the attention.

"Of course, it can also be bad," he continued, not waiting for her nonexistent answer. "In a wife, for example." He shrugged. "Every man wants a little mystery, sure. But I want to know all about the woman I'm going to spend my life with. I'm not inclined to have a relationship with an enigma."

"Good thing we're not having a relationship, then."

"Oh, but we are." His soft words seemed to drip over her like warm butter, and she licked her lips again, uncomfortable with the way her body was tingling simply from the sound of his voice.

"Excuse me?" She sat up straighter, determined that he not see he'd managed to dent her armor.

"You're my wife, remember? For the next week or so, you promised to love, honor and obey me."

Tori rolled her eyes. "I don't remember the obey part. I'm sure any ceremony we had wouldn't have included that."

"No, it did." His mouth curled into a smile. "I remember the day we discussed our vows. You were on a porch swing, wearing a flowing pink sundress."

She laughed. She had *so* never worn a sundress, much less pink.

He ignored her, continuing with his story. "And you said 'darling'—" He cleared his throat, then pitched his voice ridiculously high. "'Darling. When we marry, you'll be my master, my one and only, and I'll be your obedient little wife.'" He coughed, then took a sip from the bottle of water tucked in by the emergency brake. "Trust me. I remember it clearly."

"I'll bet you do." She crossed her arms and tried to look stern, but she couldn't quite manage it. She'd been expecting him to rub in the fact that he was leading their team, and instead he was goofing around. She hadn't expected this side of him at all, and while she was a little confused, she had to admit it wasn't unwelcome.

"I'm hurt you don't remember such an important day in our lives."

"Oh, but I do." She leaned forward, trying to concoct a story of her own.

"Exactly," he said.

"What?" She frowned. He was back to not making sense.

"*I do.* That's what you said. Those two little words are what got us into trouble."

"Ha, ha." She twisted in the seat again, then kicked her shoes off and propped her feet on the dashboard. "What I remember is that I wanted less traditional vows. You know, more modern. Husband and wife as equals. That kind of thing." She aimed an appraising look his direction. "You didn't like it at first, being basically a Neanderthal, but eventually you came around."

He kept a mostly straight face, but the tiny crinkles that appeared around his eyes told her she'd scored a few points.

"Nice to know I'm a trainable Neanderthal."

"Hell, yeah. You're very malleable. Just like putty in my hands."

"My flesh in your hands." He waggled his eyebrows. "Sweetheart, I like the sound of that."

Both his words and his low, sultry tone caught her off guard, and she had the overwhelming urge to cross her legs tightly. Suddenly her hard-earned points were slipping away. "Glad to hear it," she said, forcing bravado, "because the most we'll ever do is talk about it. No perks with this job."

"And here I'd gone and signed up for the fringe benefits. I'm sure as hell not here for my government salary."

"Then I guess I must be a huge disappointment."

"Hell, yes. Especially since this was your idea," he said. "*My* idea?"

"About getting to know each other." His voice

changed, and she recognized that they were moving from banter to work. "You're right. There's no way we can pass as a happily married couple if we don't practice. Just like you said at the airport."

Practice. She swallowed, trying to force some moisture into her mouth. She really had said that. It was number one on her list of points to address with him. And now he was praising her work. She should be thrilled. But what had seemed a reasonable plan at first now seemed dangerous. And not the kind of danger she'd anticipated when she'd joined the Bureau.

He was staring at her, gauging her reaction, and there was no way she intended to let him see that he'd thrown her. "Be careful, Sinclair." She shot him her jauntiest glance as she pulled her feet off the dashboard. "I may have taken an oath when I joined the FBI, but you can be damn sure it didn't include *that*."

Not that *that* would be all that unpleasant, but there was no way she'd ever sleep with Sinclair. She'd come close once, and look at the trouble *that* had caused.

He shifted gears, his knuckles grazing the side of her thigh. "Don't worry, agent. I'm not any more inclined to subject myself to that kind of peril on this mission than you are." He reached over and squeezed her knee. "You're safe with me."

She jumped at his touch and yanked her leg away, a stupid knee-jerk reaction that was sure to cost her, because he knew he'd really gotten under her skin.

And that, frankly, made this mission more dangerous than anything else she could have been assigned to.

CARTER HUMMED to himself as he maneuvered up Highway 101 toward Santa Barbara. Never in his wildest dreams had he expected himself to start teasing Tori. And he certainly had never expected her to respond in kind.

But he had, and she had, and the entire scenario made his head spin.

It was also a good sign.

No matter their history, and no matter any past animosity or competitiveness, first and foremost they were partners. And if there was one thing Carter believed in, it was that partners stuck together. Partners trusted each other. And, yes, partners were friends.

A few hours ago, he hadn't been certain he could hit that level of relationship with Tori. Now, though, he knew they were at least on their way.

Still, it was only baby steps. They might be getting along, but he knew Tori well enough to know that when it came time for him to pull rank, she'd likely balk.

But he'd cross that bridge when he came to it. At the moment, he had no reason to play team leader, not when her idea about spending their first few days practicing being married made so much sense.

For that matter, Tori had a lot of good ideas. Not that he'd expected anything less. Everyone at Quantico had known within minutes of meeting her that Tori had brains and drive. Carter wasn't entirely certain how Tori would perform undercover—analysis seemed to be where her real talent lay—but if there was one thing he was certain of, it was that Tori would throw herself into this assignment.

He only hoped that was a good thing. In undercover work, overzealousness could often work to your detriment. And if Tori screwed up, that meant the mission could be jeopardized. And that meant his reassignment might go out the window.

With a quick glance in her direction, he pushed the thoughts away. He had no reason to think the mission would go anything but smoothly. Positive thinking, right? The power of positive thinking would surely see him through this assignment.

"I read your report," he said.

She hooked her finger onto the bridge of her sunglasses and pushed them down her nose. "Well, yeah. I mean, I hope you weren't planning to throw yourself into this assignment without reading the background info."

Touché. "My point wasn't to tell you that I'd read it."

"Then what are we talking about?"

He tightened his hands around the steering wheel, wondering if she was intentionally baiting him. Considering the way she had her hand draped over her mouth, probably hiding a grin, he figured she was. "We're talking about your conclusions," he said. "Your report didn't really have any."

So much for light teasing. She dropped her hand, revealing a mouth set into a firm line.

"Are you nuts? Of course it did. Why do you think we're driving this highway? Because we're heading to the resort that appears to be at the center of a blackmail ring. *That* my dear Agent Sinclair, was my conclusion. And, I might add, pretty much the entire point of the report."

"All of which gets us to where we are today. But I'm wondering about when we get to the resort. Any prime suspects on your radar? The owner? Anybody?"

She glanced at him from the corner of her eye, then licked her lips.

"Tori?"

"No, not yet. I mean, I was pretty proud of myself just for making the connection to the resort."

"You should have been. Your report was impressive. In retrospect, I suppose it seems pretty obvious, but you managed to take a set of seemingly unrelated cases and find the common denominator. And considering our victims didn't exactly advertise that they'd visited a sex camp, your job wasn't all that easy."

He glanced over to see her reaction, and she was looking at him with her brow furrowed.

"What?" he said.

"I'm just wondering why you're being so complimentary."

He laughed. "Because you deserve the compliment."

"But two seconds ago you were slamming me for not including any conclusions in the report." Her mouth was tight and her back ramrod straight. The message was clear enough—Tori wasn't particularly amenable to criticism of her work.

"I wasn't slamming you. You found the connection. I was just wondering if you had any suspects."

He turned his gaze away from the road to look her in the eye, but she avoided him, turning instead to look out the side window.

"Tori?"

"What? Oh. No. I mean, that's why we're going there, right?"

Carter frowned, mentally shaking his head in exasperation. Earlier, he and Tori had seemed to be making progress, really working together as partners. But with Tori he should have known that every move would be one step forward and two steps back. "We're a team,

Lowell. If you've got your eye on someone, let me know about it."

Again, she licked her lips. But this time she didn't stay silent. "No one in particular." She nodded toward the pad in her lap. "I was just going over all the possibilities, actually. The owner's got a lot of potential, of course, since he would have contact with everyone who comes to the resort. After that..." She trailed off with a shrug.

"What?"

"Just that, the way the resort is set up, the clients follow a certain track. None of our victims line up."

"And that means what?"

"A couple of things. For one, with some of the victims, the information used to blackmail them was simply that they'd gone to the resort at all."

"The client list is confidential," Carter said. That was another reason the owner didn't make the best suspect. If word got out that the promised confidentiality had been compromised, his business would go down the tubes.

"Exactly," Tori said. "And for some of the victims, that was enough ammo to blackmail them." She riffled some papers. "For others, though..." She trailed off with a shrug. "Well, like for our celebrity victim. What celebrity would care about being seen at a sex resort?"

"So the ammo against him went a lot deeper."

Tori nodded. "Exactly. A lot nastier. A lot more provocative." She turned to face him. "And there's more. The victims didn't come in contact with the same people. Here, I'll show you." She rummaged around for a while, then pulled out a sheaf of papers with computer-generated charts and graphs. "I did this before I left. It's a breakdown of everyone we know that our victims interacted with." She pointed to the chart. "Here and here are the intersection points. But there isn't one person except the owner who came in contact with everybody."

"So maybe he is our man," Carter said. He didn't believe it, but he wondered how Tori would analyze the situation.

"Maybe." She shrugged. "Except from what I understand, he's squeaky clean."

"On the surface. Maybe underneath, he's as dirty as they come."

"Well, he certainly is the only one my research points to specifically. But still..."

"What?"

She waved the sheaf of papers. "This may suggest one result, but it doesn't feel right. He's got so much at stake. And he's such an obvious suspect."

"Too obvious?"

"I think so."

"I do, too," Carter said. He nodded toward her pile of papers. "So you just pulled that together after you were assigned this project?"

"Yeah. It wasn't hard. Research comes easy to me."

"I'm impressed." He shouldn't be, of course. Tori Lowell was one smart lady.

She flashed him a genuine smile. "Thanks."

"You'll let me know if you find any hidden clues buried in your charts and graphs?"

She laughed, revealing a tiny dimple in her cheek, then nodded. "Yeah," she said. "I promise I'll share."

While she turned to her notes, Carter whistled to himself. So far so good. Not only were they almost to Santa Barbara, but he'd made a little progress with Tori. Maybe teamwork wasn't her middle name, but at least he was pretty certain she'd make an effort. Considering it was Tori he was talking about, he considered that a victory.

Fifteen minutes later, Carter tapped the brakes, slowing the car as they passed the sign welcoming them to Santa Barbara, a quaint, Spanish-influenced town that housed a good percentage of the world's rich and famous. "Any recommendations?"

She looked up from her notes. "For what?"

"Hotels."

That must have surprised her, because she closed her portfolio and turned to face him. "We're not going straight to the resort?"

"I told you. Your idea makes sense."

She turned, facing him more directly, one eyebrow arched. "Really?"

"Really." And he wanted to make peace after their little tiff about the suspects. Not that Tori needed to know *that.* "Besides," he continued, "we're not due to meet with the task force until the day after tomorrow. They're still working on making sure our cover stories are in place. So we've got two full nights to practice being married." He grinned, then patted her hand. "Works out well, don't you think? Gives me time to get acquainted with my little wife."

She rolled her eyes. "Lesson number one—the little wife ain't so little. And she's got a mean right hook." She frowned. "So you're really agreeing to this?" She squinted, as if searching for ulterior motives.

"Hell, yes. I told you. It's perfect. You're right. But don't let it go to your head."

Her shoulders dropped a bit as she relaxed. "Well, okay, then." She aimed her blue eyes at him, and he couldn't help but smile at the light he saw there. Tori liked to win, no doubt about that. "But remember those words," she said. "I expect to hear them a lot."

"Words?"

"'You're right.'"

He laughed. "I always am."

She opened her mouth to correct him, then closed it and leaned back against her seat. "*I'm* right. You, I'm not so sure about." She flashed a grin. "But you're doing okay today."

"Thanks so much." Knowing Tori, so long as she got her way, she'd happily praise his leadership abilities.

"Anytime," she said, looking slightly smug.

"The hotel?"

"Oh." She cracked her portfolio again. "I didn't have anyplace in mind." With a shrug, she glanced at him from the corner of her eye. "Guess I wasn't really expecting you to agree."

He decided to let that one pass. "Know anything about Santa Barbara?"

"I'm an east coast girl."

"Hmm." He scanned the street, his eyes finally settling on a sign announcing tourist information. He pulled into the parking lot, stopped the car, then eased open his door. "Show time."

As they headed up the steps to the entrance, he slipped his arm around her waist. She stiffened a bit, then relaxed, and he pulled her closer, surprised at how natural she felt on his arm.

They stepped through the doors, and a ponytailed blonde looked at them. "May I help you?"

"You sure can," Carter said. He gave Tori a gentle squeeze, amused by the flash of irritation in her eye before she quelled it and turned to smile at the receptionist. "We're just passing through on the way up to the wine country. Honeymoon, you know. And we're looking for some place to spend a couple of nights."

"Newlyweds!" The young woman clapped her hands, which was a bit more reaction than Carter had been expecting. He caught Tori's eye, then shrugged in response to her slight grin.

"I just got engaged," the woman announced, holding out her hand for them. A diamond that cost more than the gross national product of a small country perched there on a platinum band.

"It's lovely," Tori said, apparently getting into their roles.

The woman's gaze dipped first to Tori's fingers, then his, and Carter cringed, realizing what was coming. "Did you decide not to exchange rings?"

Damn it. He'd left the rings in his suitcase. It hadn't occurred to him to pull them out just to run into the tourist office.

"Can you believe his brother lost them?" Tori said, jumping in to cover for him. She leaned forward, bringing this stranger into her confidence. "I was furious, of course." Then she turned and aimed a smile so wide and sweet in Carter's direction that it was all he could do to not crack up right there. "But I don't need a ring. Just my husband."

"Oh, wow. That's so sweet. I would have been spitting mad."

"She was," Carter said.

"True enough," Tori agreed. "And I've got one heck of a temper." Again, that innocent look. Only this time he detected a hint of warning. "Don't I, sweetie?"

"She certainly does."

"Still," the woman continued, "I never would have—"

"About those hotels..." Carter interrupted. He stroked Tori's shoulder with a fingertip, amused when she shivered under his touch. Probably holding back a wave of that infamous temper.

"Sure thing." The woman pulled out a binder about three inches thick, then flipped to a tab marked Lodging. "I think a bed-and-breakfast would be the most romantic, don't you?"

"Oh, I don't—"

"Perfect," Carter said.

Ten minutes later they were registered for the honeymoon package at a five room B and B on the beach. Carter even had a card for a local jeweler tucked into his back pocket. "So you can buy replacement rings," the woman had said.

"I think that went well," Carter said, as he unlocked the car and opened the door for Tori.

"Sure. Just like arranging your own execution." She slipped inside, frowning at him all the while. "Why on earth did you agree to a B and B? Do you have any idea how intimate those places are?"

"Of course I do. That's why we're there. Dress rehearsal." He didn't give her time to answer. Just shut the door and headed toward his side of the car, stopping at the trunk to rummage for their rings.

When he got inside, she was glaring at him.

He held up his hands in defense. "Hey, it was your idea."

"You're right. It was. And I hope you're memorizing your new litany—*you're right, Tori. Everything you say is right.*" She grinned. "But you know this means you sleep on the couch."

He held back a chuckle as he started the car. "Damn.

Just barely a newlywed and already I'm kicked out of the marital bed."

THEY FOUND the place easily enough. A hacienda with faded pink stucco tucked into a hill overlooking a secluded bit of the ocean.

The setting sun gave the building a warm, sensual glow, and Carter felt a twinge of regret that he wasn't really there on a honeymoon, because surely this place was made for lovers.

"Wow." Her soft whisper startled him, and Carter realized she was having much the same reaction. "It's beautiful."

He nodded, curt and firm, not wanting to reveal that his mind was already conjuring images of the two of them on the beach, in their room, in bed....

"Come on." He yanked open the door even as he yanked himself away from his sordid thoughts.

They headed into the building and were checked in by the owner's son, a lanky teenage boy who showed them to the top floor and their room.

"It's the honeymoon suite," he said, stopping outside the closed door. "Best in the house. You're lucky. Usually it's booked up, but the couple who was supposed to have it decided to come only for the weekend."

He pulled an old-fashioned skeleton key out of the front pocket of his khakis, then pushed open the door. Tori stepped through first, and he heard her gasp. She turned to face him, and he saw something unrecognizable reflected in her eyes. Wonder? Fear? He didn't know, so he followed her into the room.

As soon as he saw the layout, he knew exactly what she was thinking.

The cozy room was absolutely beautiful. A perfect lovers' paradise with one wall of windows that overlooked the ocean, a connecting bathroom featuring a claw-foot tub, a stiff-looking wing chair and, right there in the middle of the room, the one thing that had brought the gasp to Tori's lips.

A bed.

One queen-size bed draped with white netting.

An ice bucket and a bottle of champagne finished the décor.

"It's perfect," Carter said to the kid, even as his eyes continued to scan the room.

"Absolutely," Tori agreed. Her eyes caught his, and he imagined a deer caught in the headlights. He knew exactly what she was thinking, because he was thinking the exact same thing.

The room might be perfect for real newlyweds, but for them, it was anything but.

Because the room lacked one very important essential.

The room had no couch.

4

As THE KID closed the door to leave them alone, Tori fought the ridiculous urge to run after him and invite him in for a quick game of cards. Or better yet, Monopoly. Something that would take all night so she wouldn't have to deal with being alone in a room with Carter. And not just any room. No, they had to be trapped together in the most romantic room Tori had ever laid eyes on.

Not that she had a lot to compare the room to—her experience tended toward accommodations with gray metal cots and really stiff sheets—but in a room like this... Well, even she might be convinced to wear something pink and flowing.

Scary. Very, very scary.

Fortunately, Carter looked as disconcerted as she felt.

"At least there's a down comforter," Tori said. "That should pad the floor enough for you."

"For me?"

She ran her tongue over her teeth inside her closed mouth. She'd never been one to worry about chivalrous niceties. In fact, she considered the tendency of men to insist women depart an elevator first to be the height of annoyance. Half the time they had briefcases and bags and ended up creating an obstacle course when they could easily just get out of her way.

Which meant that now was not the time for her to start acting like some demure little female. If he wanted the bed, he could have the bed.

"Forget it," she said. "I'll sleep on the floor." She shot him a look. "I hope you don't snore."

"No way. You sleep in the bed—"

"No problem." If he was going to *insist*...

"—with me."

The smile that had been threatening stopped in mid-twitch. "Excuse me?"

"Something wrong with your hearing, agent?" He tossed his bags onto the bed and started unpacking, completely oblivious to the fact that she was standing across from him trying to keep a firm grip on her temper.

"There's not a damn thing wrong with my hearing, and you know it. There's nothing wrong with my temper, either. I can assure you it's in full working order."

He looked up, his expression more or less bored, damn him, then shrugged out of his shoulder holster and pitched his gun onto the bed with his clothes. "Problem, Tori?"

She inhaled, then exhaled, then inhaled again. Calm and rational. As much as it burned, he was still her superior, and for all she knew, he'd be more than happy to slam her performance in the daily reports the task force was submitting to the FBI. "My *problem*, Agent Sinclair, is that we both said *that*—" she waved toward the bed "—was something neither of us signed up for."

"Don't worry, Lowell. I don't intend to give you a second chance to walk out on me." He caught her eye. "We're only going to sleep together. Nothing more. Nothing less."

She balked, surprised he would throw that in her

face and yet somehow oddly flattered. She'd been so concerned about the fact that they'd been seen it had never once occurred to her that, perhaps, Carter had been as frustrated as she'd been embarrassed. They'd never talked about it. She'd run away, rightfully concerned about her reputation, and had spent their last week at Quantico going out of her way to avoid him.

She opened her mouth to say something, but he'd turned to his suitcase, and somehow she couldn't find the words.

As he continued to unpack, Tori recalled how his hands had felt on her that night. Her body stiffened with the memory, just as she'd stiffened when his touch at the tourist office had sent shock waves ricocheting through her. She may regret the indiscretion—and she sure as hell regretted getting caught—but she'd never once regretted his touch. No doubt about it, Carter had affected her in ways no other man ever had.

He pulled the last few items from his suitcase and threw them on the bed. Tori swallowed, trying not to pay attention, but it was hard to miss a pile of underwear stacked on the exact spot she was going to be sleeping in a few hours.

Or maybe not sleeping. Maybe it would be easier to stay awake all night.

"Boxers and briefs," he said.

Her head jerked up to meet his eyes. "Excuse me?"

He glanced to where she'd been staring. "I wear boxers *and* briefs."

She raised an eyebrow, determined to stay in control. "At the same time?"

"Very funny. Some days I go for boxers, others for

briefs." He shrugged. "Depends on my mood. And what I'm wearing."

"We have moved so far out of the realm of normal conversation I don't even know how to respond to that."

"Trust me, Lowell. I'm not telling you because I think you've got some wild underwear fetish." He nodded toward the bed and the array of clothing spread out there. "You need to know about my habits if we're going to pass as married."

She ran her hand through her hair, then twisted the end of one strand around a finger. "I hardly think anyone's going to interrogate me about your underwear."

A devious grin crossed his face. "I don't know. I've been reading up on this resort. Pretty wild stuff..."

His voice trailed off as she rolled her eyes. "And to think I never even knew this side of you existed."

"The side that wears underwear?" he asked.

He almost got her with that one, but she managed to stifle her laugh and keep a stern expression. "No, the side with the terrible sense of humor."

"Oh. That side." He grinned. "I try to keep that side hidden and fake people out by making them think I'm the next Jerry Seinfeld."

She had no idea what he was talking about, and it must have shown on her face, because he leaned forward, his hands out as if urging her to get with the program.

"Seinfeld," he said. "Great sense of humor?"

She shook her head blankly, totally lost.

"Never mind." He started putting piles of clothes into the bureau. "Your turn."

She had a feeling she knew what was coming—and she didn't like it one bit. "My turn for what?"

"Time to reveal your undies, Lowell." He nodded toward her suitcase. "Consider that an order."

She crossed her arms over her chest. "I don't think so."

"Intimacy, remember? Surely you don't want to botch this mission."

She flinched. If he'd been aiming for a target, he'd hit it. The one thing in all the world she couldn't—*wouldn't*—do was screw up. Her future was riding on it. And she intended to ace this assignment no matter what it took. But that didn't mean she was going to blindly do whatever absurd thing Carter asked. He might be her superior in name, but for practical purposes, they were peers. They'd left the academy at the same time, after all. If she were to jump just because he said boo, then it would be like admitting he'd bested her. And she wasn't about to admit that.

Besides, it wasn't as if he was giving her a serious order...

She faced him head-on. "I think sharing the bed is intimate enough. I'm not going to display my lingerie for you to ogle."

She expected him to huff and puff and cite insubordination. Instead, he flashed a curious look and said, "Why, Agent Lowell. I'm impressed."

"With what?" she countered, more than a little confused. "The fact that I know big words like lingerie and ogle?"

"Is ogle really a word?"

She propped a hand on her hip and stared him down, her jaw set.

"Okay, okay. I'm impressed that you conceded so easily."

"Conceded?"

"To sharing the bed."

That she had. "Well, you're the boss."

For that matter, although she'd razzed him, she was even going to concede the underwear point. So long as they were playing married, they might as well play it all the way. Whatever he was willing to share, she'd share that much, too...and a little bit more.

She flashed him a sweet smile—even as she aimed her gaze toward his groin. "And so long as you stay on your side of the bed, your testosterone will keep flowing. We might be playing married, but there's not going to be any consummation. You creep across the invisible line in the center, and all bets are off."

"Don't worry, agent. I don't have any intention of invading your space...." His eyes met hers, dark and dangerous, and she stifled a shiver. "Or invading anything else of yours, for that matter."

WHILE SHE STOOD THERE silently—a first for Tori—Carter congratulated himself on managing to not only get the last word, but also telling the absolute truth while doing it.

Because he had no *intention* of having sex with her—or even making an overture. No matter how enticing the proposition might be. And, truth be told, even though she'd burned him once, that particular proposition was still damned enticing.

He kept a close eye on her while he put his clothes into the top drawer of the dresser, saving the two lower drawers for Tori. When he'd tucked away his pile of underwear, he turned to her. "Well?"

"Well, what?"

"I told you. Your turn. We may have gotten a little sidetracked, but now I want to know about your undies." He managed to keep his tone serious. The truth was, he *did* need to know. He had no intention of being the least bit unprepared in the fake marriage department, and at a minimum a husband would have some idea of what his wife's panties looked like.

He turned to the dresser, supposedly to straighten his things but really needing to look somewhere other than at Tori. Even though he had a legitimate reason for seeing what his grandmother would call her unmentionables, he still had a queer feeling in the pit of his stomach—like he was out on a date and hoping to get some.

On a date, that feeling was uncomfortable enough. On an assignment, it was unprofessional, and he cursed his seeming inability to keep his mind on the job. He shook his head. No, his mind was all job. It was his body that kept wandering off into forbidden territory.

Considering the silence behind him, Carter assumed she hadn't yet come up with a snappy comeback, and he congratulated himself on stumping her. At least, he congratulated himself until he heard the distinctive sound of metal on metal as she unzipped her jeans.

Gulping air, he turned slowly, then froze at the fabulous, frustrating sight in front of him—Tori, standing there in nothing but her T-shirt and a pair of high-cut panties.

She looked at him as if she could read his mind, which, at that point, he considered a distinct possibility. "Problem, boss?"

"No problem," he lied.

"Then why are you staring? It's not like I've got anything you haven't seen before."

On the contrary. While Carter had certainly seen his

share of half-naked women, he'd never seen one that had quite the same effect on his pulse. He crossed his arms over his chest in what he hoped looked like a nonchalant gesture but was really only for the purpose of wiping his sweaty palms on his sleeves.

"Maybe I am staring," he said, figuring the best defense was a good offense. "But if I am, it's only because I never figured you for the Victoria's Secret type. I thought you'd be K-Mart all the way."

"Trust me, Sinclair. There's a lot you don't know about me."

"I'm beginning to realize that." Like how long her legs were. He'd known she'd be lean and firm—hell, she'd certainly given him a run for his money during their physical training at the academy, and that dress she'd worn on their date had been pretty damn revealing—but he'd never gotten quite this good a look. And her painted-on panties certainly weren't reducing the temptation factor. Not only that, but now that she'd taken off the cardigan she'd been wearing, he could see the outline of her bra under her white T-shirt—and damned if it wasn't trimmed in lace.

He didn't intend to touch her—not if he knew what was good for him—but that didn't change the fact that she was damned tempting. And becoming more so by the second.

"Are you finished gaping?" she asked.

"I'm not gaping."

She didn't answer. Just shot him a look that said she knew better. "For your information, my underwear's not from Victoria's Secret. Don't be a panty snob."

He held up his hands. "Sorry. I haven't had a close look at any woman's panties in quite a while. Guess my radar is off."

She quirked a brow but didn't comment. "Look, boss. It's been a long day and I'm tired. Are we working tonight or just crashing?"

He'd planned to work, but maybe going to sleep and getting a fresh start in the morning was the better plan. That would give him at least eight solid hours to let the shock of seeing Tori half-naked work its way through his body. He needed to get used to it; considering their assignment, who knew what compromising positions they'd end up in? And if his blood burned every time she stripped down or gave him a sultry look, he'd be spending more time under a cold shower than he would trying to find a blackmailer.

"Carter?" She stared at him, arms crossed. "An answer this year would be good."

"Go ahead," he said. "I've got some reading to do, and I'm not tired."

Actually, he was exhausted. But the thought of slipping into bed next to her—then lying there wide awake while he listened to her breathing and felt the bed move with each tiny motion—was a little more than he could handle right then.

"I'll stay awake with you if you want to work."

He shook his head. "I'm catching up on some other things. You go ahead. I won't be long."

That apparently satisfied her, because she grabbed a few things from her duffel, then disappeared into the bathroom. He heard the water running and tried not to imagine Tori peeling off the T-shirt and panties before she slipped into the shower.

No such luck. The image was firmly planted in his mind. Worse, even, because now he was picturing her entirely naked in the shower, her slick, soapy body enveloped in curls of steam.

He'd always known he had a good imagination—that was one of the things that made him an excellent agent, the fact that he could so easily get into someone else's head. Now, it seemed, that active imagination was determined to torment him.

The water stopped, and Carter realized he was still standing in exactly the same place, staring vaguely in the direction of the bathroom door. In about two seconds, he'd hauled himself across the room and was rummaging through his briefcase. He didn't have any catch-up reading to do, but he didn't intend to let Tori know that.

By the time she opened the door, he was sitting in the wing chair, his feet propped on an ottoman, a file filled with old reports open on his lap. A cloud of steam emerged before she did, and he knew his fantasy had been right on the money.

Wrapped in the terry-cloth robe provided by the B and B, she made her way to the bed, then cast a quick glance his way before she dropped the robe onto the foot of the bed and started to slide between the sheets wearing nothing but her T-shirt and panties. This time, though, she'd taken off the bra, and the thin cotton shirt, damp from the steamy bathroom, clung to her curves. "I, um, wasn't planning on sharing a bed," she said. "I didn't bring anything else to sleep in."

"No problem," he said, shifting the folder on his lap to better hide his body's reaction. "I didn't, either." He concentrated on his paperwork, deciding it was more prudent not to meet her eyes.

"Oh." Across the room, sheets rustled. "Well, good night." Her voice, soft and sleepy.

"Will my light bother you?"

"Uh-uh."

He glanced up and couldn't help but smile. She hadn't been kidding about being tired. Already, her eyes were shut and her breathing even. Considering that she'd left the bedside lamp on, she must have been half-asleep before she even hit the pillow.

Shaking his head, he put his folder aside and went to the bed to turn off her lamp. Before he did, though, he looked down on her. Her dark hair fanned across the pillowcase, the image all the more erotic considering how innocent her face looked in sleep.

He knew better, of course.

No matter how enticing Tori might be for a man who hadn't been with a woman in months, she was one lady he had no intention of getting involved with. For one, his playing around days were over. If he was going to bed a woman, he wanted her to be one he could build a future with. And that definitely wasn't Tori. Domesticity not only wasn't her middle name, he doubted the word was even in her personal dictionary.

Reason enough to stay away from her.

Then there were the other, more practical reasons. Like the fact that he was her superior and they were on an assignment.

And, of course, the most practical reason of all—considering the way she'd run from him years before, he knew Tori would probably prefer to eat dirt than get close to him.

All of which meant that, in a few minutes, he was to sleep with a beautiful woman—and sleep was all he was going to do.

For half a second, he considered sleeping in the chair and telling Tori he'd fallen asleep reading. But considering the chair was about as comfortable as a medieval rack, he figured she'd see through that lie pretty quickly. Which meant that, unless he wanted her to have the upper hand, he needed to crawl into that bed.

With a deep breath, he stood up. Then, knowing he probably wasn't going to get one wink of sleep, he slipped out of his T-shirt and jeans and, clad only in boxers, crawled into bed.

He made a concerted effort to stay close to the edge of the bed—and as far away as possible from the half-naked woman breathing softly beside him. Didn't matter. He was barely under the covers—his butt practically hanging off the edge—when Tori sighed in her sleep and rolled over. Toward him. And she didn't stop until her arm was draped across his chest and her bare thigh was pressed against his hip.

He held his breath, his entire body—every single inch of him—stiffening. For one brief, luxurious, decadent moment, she writhed against him, and Carter wondered if he shouldn't just roll her over, wake her up with one hard kiss and then lose himself in her sweetness.

Not the politically correct thing to do—that was damn sure—but, oh, how he wanted to.

Fortunately, Tori saved him before he reverted to a full-fledged caveman. Muttering something incomprehensible, she stilled, then fell into a deep slumber, her body warm and ripe against his.

He might be in charge of this mission, but right then, Tori had complete control of him. Lord knows, she was doing things to his body he hadn't experienced in years.

And if the warmth pulsing through his veins was any indication, it was going to be one very long, very sleepless night.

5

SO WARM...

Lost in those fitful moments before waking, Tori snuggled closer, burrowing against the solid wall of warmth that was supporting her head. *Nice.* She could stay that way forever. Safe and warm in Carter's embrace.

Carter? She froze, comprehension dawning.

Slowly she peeled open her eyes, silently praying that what she thought she'd see wouldn't really be there.

No such luck. She saw exactly what she'd feared—Carter Sinclair's naked chest. Up close, and way too personal.

Even worse, she was completely intertwined with him. Her left leg was pressed against his hip and thigh. Her right leg was draped over him, and her foot was lost somewhere underneath his knee.

And if what was going on below the waist wasn't bad enough, her arms and cheek were touching parts of Carter that she had absolutely no business exploring. Her hand was splayed out on his chest, her fingers intertwined among his smattering of chest hair while her index finger traced a jagged scar over his left breastbone. And somehow she'd ended up nestled in the crook of his arm.

The real kicker, though, was that Carter was practically balancing on the very edge of the bed. Which meant that Tori—not Carter—had maneuvered them into such an intimate position.

Damn her. She'd always been a fitful sleeper. Apparently this time she'd managed to scoot and stretch right into Carter's arms. Her head was tucked in near his shoulder, and his arm was draped across her back.

She fought the urge to lurch to her side of the bed—that would surely wake him up—and instead tried to calmly extricate herself from his embrace. Easier said than done, she realized, because as soon as she shifted her body, even slightly, his hand tightened against her back.

Frustrated, she almost gave up and went back to sleep. After all, it felt pretty nice being this close to Carter. Certainly nicer than she'd ever admit to him. Which, of course, was exactly why she had to get out of this mess before he woke up. Snuggling up and going back to sleep simply wasn't an option.

With renewed determination, she tried rolling over in his arms until she could reach his hand and peel it away from her body. He sighed, the sound deep and throaty, and she froze in mid-peel, her fingers gingerly grasping his wrist.

When he stilled, she turned her head to look at his face. Even lost in slumber, he had that determined, take-charge look that she so admired about him. No lost-little-boy look for Carter Sinclair. No, Carter was one-hundred percent male—whether asleep or awake. And that was all the more reason for her to get back to her side of the bed. She needed to be fighting the bad guys, not her attraction to her team leader.

And, of course, she *was* attracted to him. What woman wouldn't be? She might still envy his success at the academy and his later success on the job, but that didn't mean she was blind. The man was hot. But she was here to do a job—and to do it well enough that she ended up with an undercover assignment. There wasn't any way in the world she was going to sacrifice this mission because she thought Carter Sinclair looked sexy in his underwear. She'd already almost sacrificed her career because she thought he was sexy. She wasn't going to make that mistake twice.

He stirred again, and she realized with some mortification that she'd instinctively pressed closer, seeking the electricity that shot through her veins when his skin brushed against hers. Not good. Definitely not good.

She braced herself, one palm on the mattress, and started to push away from—

"Tori?"

She froze, then turned her head just enough to meet his eyes—and to see the grin reflected in those deep brown pools. "Morning," she said, hoping for a lackadaisical tone. As if she often woke up in her co-worker's arms. No big deal. Just standard operating procedure.

"And a good morning it is, too," he said. He gave her shoulder a little squeeze, his mouth twitching when she nearly jumped out of her skin.

So much for nonchalant. With one swift motion, she pushed away from him, yanking the covers up as she went, until she was standing on the other side of the bed, the sheet held in place by her arms firmly crossed over her chest. "Sorry. I must have scooted over in my sleep." She held her hands up, careful to keep her arms down to steady the sheet. "I didn't mean anything by it. Honest."

"Sweetheart, I don't doubt you for a second." He yawned, looking bored by the whole incident. Damn him. She was flustered, and he was bored. The situation not only stank, it was beginning to piss her off. She may have been the one who'd walked away years before, but she'd never quite recovered from their encounter. Carter apparently had recovered just fine.

Then he rolled his shoulders and stretched his arms, biceps and triceps and all the other -ceps from his neck to his ankles rippling as he worked the sleep out of his muscles.

She'd been wrong. She hadn't been flustered before. *Now* she was flustered.

She didn't want to stare, really she didn't, but the man was good-looking. He'd been a knockout at the academy, but he'd obviously been spending some time in the gym, and this new Carter was pretty near perfect.

He was also pretty near naked, and even though she'd had her fingers laced over his bare chest, somehow the synapses hadn't fired. Now, though, she had the sheet, and he was coverless on the bed. She'd have to be brain dead not to realize that he wasn't wearing a single thing except a pair of boxer shorts.

He turned and faced her head-on, not the least bit self-conscious. "Shall we?" he asked.

"Shall we what?"

"Not that," he said, a hint of laughter in his voice.

To her complete and utter humiliation, she realized she'd been staring at his groin. And even more humiliating was the fact that, although *her* pulse was beating at an increased tempo and her blood was flowing hotter than usual, all the evidence suggested that he wasn't the least bit turned on by her. Either that or the

man had more self-control than any other guy she'd
run across.

She ran her tongue over her teeth, then squared her
shoulders and looked him in the eye. "Believe me, I'm
not interested in *that*." She cocked her head. "So how
about dropping the innuendoes and telling me what it
is you want us to do now?"

"Practice, sweetheart," he said, sitting up and
swinging his legs over the side of the bed.

"Practice?"

"Being married. Remember? You're the little wifey."

For a second, she considered begging off and telling
him she just didn't feel up to role-playing that day. But
that was the coward's way out. This was her mission,
her plan—and her big break. And she wasn't about to
let a little thing like supercharged pectoral muscles distract her from her mission. Besides, if he could do it, so
could she.

"Fine," she said. She took a step toward him, the act
of moving psychologically sealing her resolve to be the
perfect partner...and that meant being the perfect wife.
"But if you suggest showering together, I think I'm going to draw the line."

"I'm pretty sure I can bathe myself. But if you need
some assistance..." He trailed off, his eyes flashing
bright with amusement.

Despite herself, her cheeks warmed, and she pulled
the sheet tighter, trying to maintain some shred of dig-
nity. "Thanks. I think I can manage on my own." She
nodded toward the bathroom. "Who has dibs?"

"Ladies first."

"Good." She'd showered the night before, so she
didn't really need another. But right then, more than
anything she wanted the spray to pound away the ten-

sion in her body. Not to mention a few minutes out of sight of Carter, just so she could get her head screwed on straight again. Waking up in his arms had thrown her. And it had been a long time since Tori had let anything—or anybody—get the better of her.

With her chin high, she grabbed the robe off the foot of the bed, headed into the bathroom and shut the door behind her. As soon as the door clicked into place, she sagged against the painted wood. She needed this assignment—Lord help her, she did. And she'd known it was going to be work. Hard work.

But she'd never expected that so much of the work would involve fighting her own traitorous libido. Fortunately, Tori savored a challenge. And she never, ever lost.

She frowned, mentally correcting herself. *Except once.* Her rank at the academy. And, damn it all, she'd lost to Carter Sinclair.

As soon as Tori disappeared into the bathroom, Carter let his entire body relax. Fortunately, he'd awakened before her, which meant he'd had time to wrest his body into some semblance of control.

He'd spent the twenty minutes before she stirred thinking of mundane things like paperwork and car repairs and whether or not he'd remembered to send in the rebate form for the digital camera he'd purchased last week. By the time she stirred against him, his monster erection had been history.

Thank God. The last thing he wanted on this mission was for Tori to think she had gotten the best of him.

The shower stopped, and he heard the clackety-clack of the curtain being pulled back. Any second now, she was going to open that door and find him still sitting there like a lump wearing nothing but his boxer shorts.

Under the circumstances, probably not the best scenario, so he headed to the bureau and rummaged through his things until he found the T-shirt he'd worn yesterday. He grabbed his folder of mission notes and sat on the side of the bed just as the bathroom door opened.

She emerged from the mist like some ethereal apparition. He'd noticed last night, of course, but, damn, the woman looked good in a bathrobe. In reality, the fluffy terry-cloth contraption probably had more material than jeans and a turtleneck—but the image of her bundled in the soft white material was surprisingly erotic.

Enough already. Get with the program. He gave himself a mental wallop even as he focused on the file folder in his hand. He needed to keep his mind on the mission, not on ridiculous thoughts about his partner.

Unfortunately for Carter, today the assignment called for him to learn more about Tori. As a woman. As a *wife.* He needed to know her intimately, and the prospect was both exciting and unnerving.

Once again, he wondered what the hell he'd gotten himself into.

"Jockey," she said, facing him.

"What?" He blinked, his frazzled brain trying to form some synapse that might clue him in to what she was talking about. Nothing came to mind.

"You wanted to talk about my underwear." She held up a pair of black panties. "I wear Jockey. For women, of course."

"Of course," he muttered. He wasn't sure if she was trying to cooperate on their plan to prepare or if she was trying to bait him. Didn't matter. He didn't intend to be baited, and they did have to prepare. "Mine are Jockey, too," he added.

She lifted her eyebrows. "Well, well. To think we actually have something in common."

"A solid foundation for our marriage," he said, then chuckled. Even though working with Tori wouldn't have been his first choice, at least he knew it would never be dull.

"I've got a birthmark on my butt," she said.

Yup. Never dull. "And you're telling me this because..."

"Intimacy, remember?" Her fingers snaked through the belt of the robe, poised to pull it open and reveal all.

Carter swallowed. She was definitely baiting him. And, damn her, considering the way every little atom in his body was starting to burn, odds were she was going to win this round.

"If you need to see it..."

"Not necessary, agent," he growled far too quickly, but he needed to get out of there. "I believe you." He took a step toward the bathroom. "And it's my turn."

"It certainly is. What have you got on your butt?"

He paused mid-step, not turning around until he was sure his expression wouldn't reveal that she was getting to him. "My turn for the bathroom," he finally said. Then he headed straight into the steam-filled room, the amused expression on her face still burned into his brain. She'd won this round, and she knew it. Despite all his talk about how they needed to plan for the mission—to get to know each other intimately for professional purposes—in the end, he'd been the one who'd had to escape because the talk turned to panties and rear ends.

Tori one, Carter zip. But that was okay. In the end, only the mission mattered. And he didn't intend to fail on that count.

He turned on the shower, letting it run while he shaved. As more steam filled the room, he noticed the scent of lavender. He frowned, wondering where it came from, and then he caught sight of the bottle of body lotion sitting on the small table next to the tub.

Tori's lotion. He picked it up, holding it close to his nose. As he breathed in the feminine scent, he was struck by the dichotomy between Tori the agent and Tori the woman.

He was attracted to the woman; hell, what man wouldn't be? But the agent? Well, unless she'd changed, Tori's get-out-with-guns-blazing I'll-do-anything-to-distract-the-competition attitude irritated the hell out of him.

Still, as he climbed into the shower, he had to admit that so far she'd been the perfect partner. She'd brought good ideas to the table, and her one overly aggressive not preauthorized caper—calling the newspaper—hadn't done any harm.

So maybe she'd changed. Maybe Tori wasn't a liability, after all. Maybe *he* was. Him and this damned attraction that was going to get him into trouble if he didn't rein it in.

Unless...

Mentally, he slapped himself on the head. A true V-8 moment; why hadn't he seen it before? He didn't need to hide his attraction—he needed to play it up.

In just over twenty-four hours he and Tori were going to check into a sex camp. They'd spend the next few days posing as a couple who'd paid a small fortune to learn how to spice up an already spicy sex life.

They needed sexual tension, all right. They needed it in spades.

So the fact that he was attracted to Tori wasn't a bad thing. Hell, for all she knew, he was simply playing his role as the horn-dog husband and not the spurned and frustrated man she'd walked out on at Quantico. And rather than let Tori think she'd somehow gained the upper hand in their professional relationship, that was going to be his story.

As soon as he got to that bedroom, he was going to make sure Tori looked at *him* with an equal amount of lust in her eyes. Yes, indeed. He wanted to see lust in her eyes, and no running away. And he'd make it an order if he had to.

A pounding at the door pulled him from his reverie, and he shut off the water. "What?" he called.

"Just wondering if you'd drowned in there."

"I like long showers."

"Got it. Long showers. Jockey. Boxers *and* briefs. But not at the same time." She paused, and he imagined her grin. "How am I doing so far, boss?"

"You're my prize pupil." He pulled a towel from the rack and wrapped it around his hips, only then realizing that he'd left his change of clothes in the bedroom. Well, damn. He could climb into his boxers or he could brave the next room—and the woman in it—and go get clean clothes.

His hand hesitated on the doorknob. Then he sucked in a breath and turned. What the hell. They were supposed to be married, right?

Her eyebrow quirked as he stepped into the room, but she didn't say anything.

He headed for the chest of drawers, opened it and

pulled out a pair of navy blue briefs. "So, are you ready?"

"To watch you drop that towel?" Her eyebrow was still riding high, but her voice was cool and crisp. "I don't think so."

He stifled a grin. She might be playing it cool, but she couldn't hide the hint of nervousness. Well, good. Lord knows he was on edge being around her. If him wandering around in a towel evened the score, then he was prepared to spend the next week wearing nothing but a monogrammed loincloth.

"Problem, agent?" he asked, turning to face her.

"No problem." Her gaze drifted toward his groin. "But unless you've hidden the blackmailer's identity under there, I don't think I need to see what that towel's hiding."

He chuckled and headed for the closet. "Hell of a way for a married couple to live."

"We're not married."

"No, but this is our dress rehearsal, remember?"

She crossed her arms over her chest. "Sinclair, if watching you put on underwear is crucial to our mission success, then you go right ahead. I'm pretty sure I won't be so overcome by libidinous thoughts that I ravage you on the spot."

"Damn," he said, aiming a wolfish glance her direction. "And here I thought I was irresistible."

"Wrong again, hotshot."

He shook his head. "No way, sweetheart. I'm right on the money."

She blinked. "Excuse me?"

"You're attracted to me."

She shook her head. "Maybe once. Maybe a long time ago. But not anymore."

He frowned, surprised at her response and wondering if she really had felt some attraction at Quantico. But, no. He knew better. She'd never been attracted to him. It had all been a ruse to try and throw him off his game. He looked her in the eye, determined to get on with his plan and not let her attempts to soothe his ego throw him. "You're desperately in love with me," he said, his voice firm.

"Did the steam melt your brain? I'm—"

"My bride. Remember?"

He could hear her exhale from across the room.

"Right," she said. "Of course. We're..." She made a twirling motion with her hand.

"About as hot for each other as two people can be." He finished the thought for her. "After all, that's the reason we're stuck together in a honeymoon suite, right?"

The look she aimed at him was cold enough to melt ice, but she nodded. "You're right. Change wherever you want. We may as well get Operation Orgasm underway."

"Operation Orgasm?"

A grin tripped across her lips. "Catchy, don't you think?"

"It has a certain ring to it." He turned, keeping his back to her as he dropped his towel, then pulled on his briefs and slacks. When he turned back, she was staring right at him as if he'd done nothing more unusual than reset his alarm clock. Well, why should he expect more? He didn't believe she'd ever really been attracted to him—not at the academy and not now.

For years, Tori Lowell had seen him as one thing and one thing only—competition. Now, with this assignment, maybe she saw him as a stepping stone to a better position. But as a man? He'd learned the hard way that Tori had never really been interested in him as a man, and he had no reason to think she'd start now.

Even though he knew it shouldn't, her obvious lack of interest bothered him. He told himself it was merely ego run amok. Certainly he wasn't *disappointed* in her lack of interest. Tori might be a beautiful woman, but she wasn't his type. He'd admit to lust, but nothing more.

But even that irked because there was no doubt in his mind that any real attraction between them was, once again, purely one-sided. The fact she'd so cavalierly named their assignment only underscored that, to Tori, nothing about this mission was real. If she acted like she was attracted to him, it was because she was playing a role. That's all. Nothing more. Nothing less.

He'd do well to emulate her in that respect.

He grabbed his shirt from the top of the dresser and shrugged into it, his fingers attacking the buttons. "Are you ready?"

"Ready?" A shadow crossed her face that he couldn't read.

"Yeah. To start Operation Orgasm." He finished the buttons and started tucking in his shirt. "Are you ready?"

"Oh. Right. Of course. Of course I'm ready."

"You're sure?" She seemed distracted somehow, but he couldn't put a finger on what about her was bugging him. "Because today's our one full day of dress rehearsal. When we go down those stairs, I want everyone we bump into thinking that we could jump each other at any moment."

"Don't worry," she said, her blue eyes as chilled as

her voice. "I can play make-believe with the best of them."

But while her voice might be icy, her cheeks were flushed. Warm. And Carter had to wonder if maybe she wasn't as detached as she wanted him to believe. Perhaps there was a hint of attraction on her end, as well.

And if that was the case...

He hid a private smile, and his damn ego jumped for joy.

6

"WOULD YOU LIKE another biscuit, dear?" Phyllis Rafferty, their hostess, smiled as she passed a basket under Tori's nose.

The yeasty fragrance tempted, but Tori held up a hand and pushed back from the table. "I couldn't possibly. I've already had two." She glanced at Carter, then took his hand, hoping she looked like an excited bride—as opposed to an undercover agent trying to look like an excited bride. "We're going down to the beach, and I don't want to sink like a rock to the bottom."

The woman smiled. "You're not from California, are you, dear?"

"Virginia. I work in Washington. Why?"

"The Pacific's cold. Even in August." Phyllis spread her smile between Tori and Carter. "If you want to take a swim, I suggest you use the pool. We keep it heated. And the hot tub is private. Just flip the sign over and close the gate. None of the other guests will bother you."

Carter squeezed her hand as Phyllis started explaining where the controls for the heat and bubbles were located. While the older woman talked, Carter leaned over to kiss Tori's cheek. She leaned into the kiss, a smile plastered on her face even as she fought the urge to kick him under the table. He was intentionally taunting her, and she wondered if he'd caught her looking at him with more than just professional detachment.

When he'd dropped that towel, and she'd gotten an eyeful of his Mel Gibson-quality rear, it had taken every bit of acting skill she possessed to keep from staring and drooling. She'd tried to school her features into a cool, uninterested expression, but who knew if she'd succeeded?

It irked her that she still found him so attractive. But the truth was the truth. He was hot, and she'd come damn close to revealing she thought so. Had she come closer than she'd realized? Had he noticed?

She gnawed on her lower lip. No, his back had been to her, and she'd been careful to keep any signs of interest out of her voice. So this current flirting was nothing more than Carter playing his role. And if he could, then so could she.

"—and that's all you have to do to work the timer," Phyllis was saying.

With a little toss of her hair, Tori leaned over and hugged Carter, aiming for a performance worthy of an Academy Award nomination. "Oh, darling! The hot tub sounds fabulous. Can we?" Mentally, she rolled her eyes. The only award the academy would give her would be the one for overacting.

He brushed a soft kiss along her cheek, and she shivered despite herself. "Sweetheart, we can do anything you want to do."

Phyllis beamed, as if she'd personally introduced them and was now basking in the glory of their marriage. Clearly, the woman loved opening her home to newlyweds, and for a moment Tori felt a twinge of guilt for the ruse they were pulling.

"So what do you do in Washington?" Phyllis asked, topping off Tori's coffee.

"She's an accountant," Carter said, answering before she could open her mouth.

"I work for a small firm that does a lot of litigation support," she added, glaring at him. What did he think? That she'd forget her cover story? She might not have his experience in the field, but she was just as competent as he was. "Forensic accounting," she added. "You know, going after the bad guys."

"Like *Murder, She Wrote*, only with numbers," Phyllis said. She pulled out a chair and sat across from them. "How fascinating."

Tori met Carter's eyes, and she could tell he was holding in laughter, just like she was. "Well, I never thought of it that way," Tori said. "But, yeah. I guess you're right."

Hell, the way Phyllis talked, her former job sounded almost as exciting as working at the FBI. Of course, considering she'd been holed up at a desk at the Bureau, too, the jobs weren't all that dissimilar.

"And what do you do?" Phyllis turned her attention to Carter.

"He's a firefighter," Tori said, neatly sideswiping Carter's answer just like he'd done hers. For their cover stories, they'd planned to use their old jobs, before they'd joined the FBI. But Carter had been a cop, and since that might have made the bad guys nervous, they'd fudged on his job. Now he was a firefighter.

Tori only hoped Carter'd had time to study up on the profession enough that he could talk the talk and walk the walk.

"A fireman! How wonderful." Phyllis leaned toward them. "My nephew Eldon is a fireman in Atlanta.

He's on leave right now recovering from an injury he received from a..." She paused, and her finger went to her temple. "What do you call that thing you use to pry things open?"

Tori held her breath.

"You mean a halligan tool," Carter said, sounding for all the world like he kept one or two of the gizmos in his back pocket.

Tori exhaled, silently cursing herself. She should have known Carter would be up to speed on his new career. The man did nothing half-assed.

The thought made her shiver. She was about to be romanced, albeit pretend, by a man who never skimped on an assignment. What would he do? And, more important, how would she react? She shivered again, remembering the way his chest had felt under her fingers, that jagged scar beckoning for her to kiss it and make it better.

Even now, she could still remember the way his hands felt as he'd caressed her shoulders so many years ago. And the way his lips had burned on hers, his mouth warm and demanding. His tongue seeking entrance. She clung to the memory, wondering if she'd ever again feel like that in the arms of a man. And if she wouldn't ever feel that way for real, was it okay to pretend with Carter?

She cringed at her foolish thoughts, wishing she could turn the lust off. Impossible, of course. Even with all her self-control and training, it would still be hiding under the surface, revealing just enough to torment her.

She sighed. Too bad people didn't come with on-off buttons.

"You must be very proud of him," Phyllis said, pulling Tori back to the real world. "Firemen are truly heroes."

Tori nodded, then steeled herself as she took Carter's hand, his flesh warm against hers. She smiled at Phyllis. "I'm very proud."

"Have you ever been injured?" Phyllis asked, turning her attention to Carter.

"Just once, ma'am. I, uh, got caught by a falling beam. Got me right across the chest."

"It's healed, of course," Tori said. "But he'll always have that scar."

"You poor thing," Phyllis said, even as Carter turned to stare at Tori, a bemused expression on his face.

In a flash, she realized her mistake. When he'd awakened that morning, she'd pulled away, trying to give the impression she'd just woke up, as well. Certainly, she hadn't wanted him to realize she'd been lying there while the sun rose, her head resting against him as she inspected every visible inch of his body.

So much for that little ruse.

"And what do you two lovebirds have planned for the day? Besides the hot tub, that is."

"Talking," Carter said, a curious expression still reflected in his eyes. "And long walks on the beach."

Phyllis beamed at them. "How romantic."

Tori silently agreed. On any other day, with any other man, the scenario would be romantic. As it was, they were going to be grilling each other, trying to cram all the details of their supposedly sexually stimulating marriage into one afternoon at the beach.

She pressed her thighs together, the prospect of an afternoon sex chat making her tingle. Talk about a dangerous assignment. There were times when her government salary really wasn't enough.

But she needed the time with Carter, needed the practice. She might be desperate for an undercover assignment, but she wasn't stupid. Carter had years of experience on her. And while she might have more classroom savvy than anyone she'd ever met, she still wasn't sure she could live up to her father's reputation in the field. Or, for that matter, to Carter's.

She wanted the job—had been working her whole life for it, in fact—and yet she still had those curl-up-under-the-covers moments where she really didn't know if she was good enough. She hated that part of herself. The unsure, scared part, and she'd spent her whole life proving to everyone that she was good enough. So far, she'd managed to prove it to everyone but herself. Everyone, that is, except the powers that be at the FBI. They were punishing her for one stupid mistake.

Except...

She frowned. There were times when she wondered if her job assignment had nothing to do with Carter. If it was all her. If she'd somehow failed and didn't even know it. If she really wasn't good enough, and her superiors knew that.

No. She was thinking foolish thoughts simply because she was scared. She sat up straighter, determined to shake off the fear and insecurity. Because that was a part of her she'd never—never—let Carter see.

Phyllis pushed back from the table. "Now, you two run along and change, and I'll pack you a lunch to take with you." She winked. "Something suitable for newlyweds."

True to her word, by the time Tori and Carter had

changed into shorts and sandals, Phyllis had filled a backpack with soft cheeses, wine and fruit. Carter hoisted it over his shoulder, then slipped an arm around Tori's waist and steered her toward the back door. "Ready?" he asked.

She nodded. "Ready."

But, she wondered, ready for what?

"SO WE'LL LEAVE tomorrow?" Tori asked.

Carter nodded. They were on the beach, about fifty yards from Phyllis's back door, walking hand-in-hand through the surf. He looked over his shoulder, and Phyllis, their enthusiastic innkeeper, waved. "That's the plan," he said. "Today and tonight we'll have a crash course on each other, tomorrow we'll head out and meet up with the rest of the task force, and tomorrow afternoon we'll check in at the resort."

"And we're booked for a week? Do you think that will be long enough?"

He flashed a wicked grin and squeezed her hand. "I thought you told me you'd have this thing solved by today." He leaned closer, using his best *Saturday Night Live* Wild and Crazy Guy voice. "If that's the case, we're just going to the resort to relax and enjoy."

She scanned him up and down. "Sweetie, I've seen your backside, and if we're only going to have a good time, I think I'll take a rain check."

The twinkle in her eye took the sting out of her words, and he returned fire with a grin as they walked along. "And what's the matter with my butt?"

Her cheeks flushed, but she squared her shoulders and looked him straight in the eye. "Carter, there are certain things women look for in a man's butt. You just don't have it." She tugged her hand free. "Sorry, but I guess you had to fail at something in your life."

Her words came out as a joke, but he knew better. In Tori's mind, Carter had never failed at anything. And now he had one-upped her again. After all, he was leading the task force, not her, and he could imagine how much that irked her. Especially since she'd gone to so much trouble to try and distract him from their final tests at the academy.

Well, too bad. Carter had one shot at getting his reassignment, and he didn't intend to let Tori's petty little jealousies screw that up. Reaching out, he snagged her hand again, pulling her close to him.

"Excuse me?"

"We're madly in love, remember?"

She turned to face him, her features tight. "How could I forget?" Once again, she pulled her fingers free. "But the beach is deserted. I think we can drop the visuals while we talk about our stellar love life."

He took her hand again. "No, sweetheart, we can't."

"Damn it, Sinclair, I'm not your little wind-up dolly." She jerked her hand free and glared at him. "If you want to talk, we'll talk. But I'm not playing prom night with you."

No, Carter imagined that she wouldn't. All the evidence made it perfectly clear Tori didn't want anything to do with him unless they were on display or unless it suited her specific purposes.

For about two seconds, he considered arguing with her and pushing the point. But he knew that arguing with Tori would be futile. No, Tori insisted on getting her own way. And unless he grabbed control and held on tight, he'd never really be in charge of this assignment.

He took her hand again. "Sorry, babe."

"Are you deaf?"

This time, as she jerked away, he caught her by the shoulders. "You're right. Who needs to hold hands?" Before she could pull away, he spun her around, wrapping one arm around her waist. Their hips meshed together, and he pressed against her, already hard just from the few seconds of contact.

She gasped, her eyes wide, and he took advantage of her surprised little "oh" to close his mouth over hers.

At first her mouth was hard and firm, unyielding to his explorations. But he refused to relent, tasting and teasing, his tongue warring with hers until she relaxed. She moaned, a low noise deep in her throat, as her lips softened against his.

He stroked her back, his fingers delighting in her softness even as his mouth tasted her sweetness. For one brief, incredible moment, they simply shared the pleasure. Not undercover, not rivals, not colleagues. Just Tori and Carter on a beach.

She stiffened, and reality returned. Her fingers closed tight on his shoulders as she pushed away, her eyes flashing with raw anger. "What the hell do you think you're doing?" Her measured words punctuated the brisk sea air.

"My job, sweetheart." He allowed himself one small grin. "And I have to say, this job may not be so bad, after all."

"Your job? Your *job?*" Her hands went to her hips. "Your job is to accost me?"

"My *job*, sweet stuff, is to be your lover, remember? And that's exactly what I intend to be."

"Oh. Oh, I see." Her eyes narrowed, and then she popped off a salute. "Well, yes sir, Mr. Boss Man, sir."

She reached up and unbuttoned her shirt, then slipped her sleeve off her shoulder. She followed with the other sleeve, then shrugged out of the garment until she was standing there in a bikini top, staring him down.

Carter raised an eyebrow but held his tongue, half of him desperate to know what she was going to do next, the other half dreading it.

"If that's the way you want to play it," she said. Her hands slipped behind her neck, and she untied the string holding her top. Down it came, lower and lower, until those two little triangles of material were just about to reveal—

"Hold it," Carter said, holding up a hand even as he cursed himself for wimping out. It would serve her right if he let her strip completely naked. But that wasn't the way he wanted to run this assignment, and that certainly wasn't the way to get off on the right foot with Tori.

"But we're lovers, remember?" She nodded toward the ground. "Shall we just drop down here and go for it? The beach is relatively deserted. I figure only one or two people will see us doing the wild thing."

"I'm getting a definite disapproval vibe here. I'm guessing you didn't like the kiss."

She touched her nose. "Bingo."

"Got your attention, though, didn't I? Considering you seemed more than willing to drop your cover the second we were out of Phyllis's sight, I thought it was necessary."

With a scowl, she tied the top around her neck, then slipped her shirt over her shoulders. "For future reference, you can get my attention just by calling my name."

"I'm not so sure." He took her hand and gave a

slight tug as they headed down the beach. "This," he said, squeezing her hand, "is all I actually wanted. Just a simple gesture to keep up appearances. But you seemed determined to act like we're in fifth grade and I have cooties."

Her eyes widened. "You mean you *don't* have cooties?"

"Tori..." He laced his voice with a warning note.

"I'm sorry." She licked her lips. "You're right."

He stopped walking and turned to face her. "Would you mind repeating that?"

"Yes, as a matter of fact, I would. You heard me the first time."

"I did. I just couldn't believe my ears."

She shot him an annoyed glance. "I apologized. What more do you want me to say?"

"That you're going to play this straight. That you're not going to screw up this mission." He was pushing, and he knew it. But the woman was a powder keg, and Carter wasn't about to risk her messing up this assignment for him. "I need this mission to go down perfectly. And I need to know that you're behind me all the way."

"Of course I am." Her brow furrowed. "You may think you have a lot riding on this assignment, but I have *everything*. This is my ticket out of some damned cubbyhole. Maybe you managed to come away from our little tryst unscathed, but I didn't."

He frowned, not understanding what she was talking about, but she continued before he had a chance to ask.

"I want an undercover assignment so badly I can taste it. Do you really think I'd screw it up?"

She had a point. "Fair enough," he said. "Just keep

in mind that an undercover operative is undercover all the time. Not just when the spotlight is on."

She cocked her head. "So we're madly, passionately in love all the time. Not just when Phyllis is looking or when the resort folks are doing their thing."

"Exactly."

She shrugged. "I can live with that."

He remembered the way her body had been pressed up against him that morning in bed. Maybe she could live with that, but right then, Carter had to wonder if he could. He'd just insisted that a woman who made him harder than he'd been in a long time treat him as a lover twenty-four hours a day. Right then, he didn't know if the assignment was getting better...or worse.

7

WHEN THEY'D SET OUT, the sun had been on the rise, beating down as they walked along the secluded beach. Now it was starting to descend, and the ocean breeze was turning cooler.

Carter almost couldn't believe it. He'd spent the past six hours with Tori and, except for a bit of a rocky beginning, they were getting along just fine. Hell, for that matter, they were actually working, and she was doing her damnedest to learn her part as the sex-kitten wife who'd talked her husband into exploring all the Kama Resort had to offer.

Carter's body stiffened. He had no idea what was in store for him when they reached the resort, but he was positive it would be...interesting. *How* interesting he didn't know, but he had only himself to blame. He could have picked Door Number Two, and they could be pretending to be sexually dysfunctional. The resort director would pat their heads and send them to their room to try something easy like massage therapy.

But no. In a fit of hubris, he had to suggest that they pretend to be a couple who'd already qualified for the sexual Olympics, and now they were going for the gold. Forget basic massage...from what Carter had read about the resort, they'd be enrolled in a Tantric sex class before Carter could say boo.

Even under normal circumstances, Carter was pretty

sure that Tantric sex wasn't on his top ten list. He sure as hell didn't want to be exploring it with the likes of Tori.

"Carter? Are you even listening to me?" Tori tugged on his hand.

"Sorry. My mind's wandering. What?"

"I asked if you were really nineteen."

He shrugged. "Too old or too young?"

"I guess I just assumed someone like you would have...you know..." Her hand twisted in the air. "Explored your sexuality a little earlier."

"Someone like me?"

Her face flushed pink, and Carter fought the urge to trace his thumb along her cheekbone. "It's just that you're attractive," she said.

"Thanks," he said.

"Don't thank me. I didn't pick your chromosomes." Her words were nonchalant, but he knew she was embarrassed. She'd let on that she'd noticed him. Not Carter the boss, but *him*. And that must be driving her nuts.

"Anyway," she continued, "in my experience, the good-looking guys tended to know it...and flaunt it."

"Yeah, well, I was only interested in exploring with Amy Lindbarger, and she wanted to wait."

"So how was it?"

"I thought it was great. But Amy must have disagreed since the next day she dumped me for Brad Keaton. They're married now. Five kids."

"That sucks," she said.

"No. They're nice kids." He aimed a smile her direction.

She bopped him lightly on the arm. "I meant the dumping you part."

"Yeah," he agreed. "That did suck. But it taught me a valuable lesson."

"Don't postpone having sex?"

"Something like that." Carter took a step closer, the floral scent of her body lotion tickling his nose. "It's a lesson I live by even now." He took her hand, his thumb caressing her smooth skin. "I go after what I want when I want."

"And what do you want?"

Carter didn't know if it was his imagination, but her breath seemed to hitch. "I want this assignment to come off without any glitches." He took a step closer, trying to control his breathing, fighting the urge to touch her all over. "I'm glad we're working together, Tori. I really am."

He'd debated saying that, even if it was the truth. Her edges might be raw, but her drive and her talent were real.

"Thank you," she said, her voice sincere but laced with a note of surprise.

They walked in comfortable silence until he nodded toward a hot dog stand on the boardwalk up ahead. "Hungry?"

"Starved, actually."

They hurried to the stand in silence, and he ordered them each a dog with the works.

"I know what I want out of this assignment," she said after they were settled on a bench with their food. "But what about you? Why is this such a big deal for you?"

For a moment, he considered avoiding the question. But they'd been getting along, really talking, and he didn't want to pull back now. She'd notice the distance, and it might impact their assignment. They were supposed to be intimate, and in Carter's mind, that meant mentally as well as physically.

"Carter?" she prompted.

"I want out."

"Of the Bureau?" Disbelief rang in her voice.

"No. I love the FBI. I just don't want to pull another undercover assignment."

Her forehead creased. "But you're such a good agent."

He laughed. "I can be a good agent behind a desk, too. And I can be out in the field without being undercover."

From her expression, he could tell she didn't agree, but she didn't argue. He supposed her incredulity made sense. After all, her father's escapades as an undercover agent had become legend. Even after Lowell had gotten married and had Tori, he still took undercover assignments. It must have been hell on Tori's home life, but apparently she hadn't been too scarred, since she seemed determined to follow in her old man's footsteps.

"But why be behind a desk if you could pull an undercover assignment?"

"Maybe undercover work's not all it's cracked up to be."

She shook her head. "Nah. That I don't believe."

"I didn't figure you would."

She raised a brow. "Somehow, I think I've just been insulted."

He sighed. "All I'm saying is that you can be a good agent without being undercover. Real life's out there. With families and mortgages and hamsters. Don't want this job so badly that you forget that."

"Hamsters?"

He shrugged. "You know what I mean."

"Don't worry about me," she said. "I'm more than capable of taking care of myself."

"I figured that out years ago," he said. A shot of anger burst through him, and he worked to tamp it down. He was being foolish. The past was the past, and he needed to move beyond it.

Resolved, he stood up, tossing his napkin into a trash can before holding his arm out for her. "This is all beside the point. Tell me about you."

"Me? I still want the undercover job."

"No," he said. "How old were you when you finally lost it."

"It? Oh, we're back to *it*." She twined her arm around his waist as they walked along the sand, heading toward the private beach behind Phyllis's B and B. "And just what makes you think I don't still have it?"

"I—" He closed his mouth, suddenly unsure whether she was joking. Tori Lowell, a virgin? Surely not.

"Not sure, are you?" She danced ahead, her eyes bright. "What do you know? I'm an enigma."

"But one I'm happy to find the answer to."

She skipped toward him, stopping to pull off her sandals. "Find?" she asked, kicking her toes in the surf. "Are you saying you expect me to tell you? Or are you planning to, uh, dig for buried treasure?"

She was joking, of course, but at the moment, the thought didn't seem so ridiculous. The Tori he was getting to know wasn't the Tori he'd expected when he'd first been assigned this case. And he had to say he liked the woman he was getting to know. Liked her too much for his own good, probably.

Hell, he knew better than anyone that getting close

to Tori Lowell could be dangerous. But then, what was the point of being an FBI agent if you didn't face a little danger now and then?

Determined, he stepped closer. "You know," he said, "we are supposed to be lovers." Her eyes widened, and he stifled a grin. "Maybe I *should* see what kind of treasure I can find." He took another step in her direction.

"Or maybe not," she said, taking a step backward. The sun was beginning to set, and the orange-and-purple sky surrounded her like a backdrop.

"No? You're the one who suggested it. Just like you suggested we practice being married." He took another step toward her as she took another step back. Carter stifled a grin, amused to realize he'd found a chink in her armor "I don't know, Tori. Maybe this is what you had planned all along."

"This? Exactly what are we talking about?"

"Sex, agent. We're talking about sex." He aimed a wicked grin her direction as he wondered how she'd extricate herself from this one—and what he'd do if she *didn't* extricate herself. "We're a young couple in love, right? And as team leader, it's my job—no, my *duty*—to make sure we're convincing in the parts."

TORI SWALLOWED, not at all certain whether he was joking or not. Surely he didn't really intend for them to sleep together. Being consistently on when doing undercover work made perfect sense. But she couldn't imagine that Carter really expected them to have sex simply because they needed to stay in character.

Did he?

Dragging her teeth over her lower lip, she turned toward the surf. In truth, losing herself in Carter's embrace was tempting. Very, very tempting. And she wanted what he was offering more than she cared to admit, and certainly more than she should considering the price she'd paid the last time she'd succumbed to his arms.

But even though she wanted it, she wasn't at all sure he was really offering. Most likely, he wasn't serious. After all, there were laws about bringing sex into the workplace. And no matter how intense an undercover job might be, suggesting that sex came with the territory was just a little too much.

With any other agent, she'd know he was joking and simply laugh it off. With Carter, though...

They had a history. She'd run out on him. And now he had the upper hand. Was he intending to use it to get her into bed?

"Tori?"

Still not sure what to do, she decided that the best defense was a good offense. The possibility that somehow Carter was winning their little game simply wouldn't do. "What's the matter, Sinclair? Are you questioning your skill as an undercover agent?"

"Excuse me?"

She stepped closer. "Can't you pretend to be wildly passionate about me *without* the sex?" She swung an arm around his neck. "I know I can. Want me to show you?"

Without waiting for his response, she pulled herself up and pressed her lips to his. She was tall, but he was taller, and she had to balance on her tiptoes to hold the kiss. At first, he seemed surprised, but his mouth soon hardened under hers, and his arm closed around her waist and pulled her close.

Her knees went limp, and she realized it was a good

thing he was holding her up. He'd kissed her earlier, when they'd first set out from Phyllis's, and the feel of his lips against hers had sent a warm rush surging through her body. She'd wanted more, but he'd pulled away.

Now, though…now she intended to take what she wanted. With a little sigh, she hooked one hand around his neck, her fingers splayed up the back of his head. His coarse short hair teased her fingers as she explored, the sensation of his hair gliding over her skin while his tongue warred with hers blatantly erotic.

He groaned, low and masculine, as he pulled her closer. She opened her mouth, silently urging him to take even as she gave and surprising herself by how much more she wanted from this man.

He deepened their kiss, and she reciprocated, exploring his mouth with her tongue, tasting and teasing. His flavor was just what she'd remembered—male and raw and delicious. His upper lip was scratchy from his evening beard, and it grated against the soft flesh of her lip, the sensation both erotic and somehow comforting.

The musky scent of aftershave layered over the clean smell of soap tickled her nose. The combination was uniquely Carter, and she breathed deep, wanting to memorize his scent.

With a gentle nip on her lower lip, he broke the kiss, his mouth moving to graze her ear even as his hands eased under her shirt, his fingertips tickling her back as he traced the length of her spine. Up and down, his languid movements set off a chain reaction, sending shock waves racing through her body.

She knew she needed to end this, to not let it go any further. Even more, she wanted to end it before he did.

She wanted to be the one calling the shots, the one in charge. If not of the mission, then at least she could control this—whatever *this* was.

But somehow, she couldn't pull away. Not right then. Not when every soft stroke of his hand sent spurts of fire zipping to the ends of her fingers and toes. She could only give in and enjoy the sensation, both wicked and welcome.

With one hand, he pulled her closer, and she moaned, the sound turning into a gasp when his fingers slipped under the waistband of her shorts. The touch was far from intimate, but the boldness of it struck her. She wanted his touch. Right then, she wanted it more than anything she'd ever wanted, and she silently willed him to continue his erotic exploration. When his hand slowed, coming to rest at the base of her spine, she forced herself not to cry out in frustration and beg him to continue.

She couldn't ask, not out loud. But she could take, and with a firm tug, she released his tucked-in shirt. She pushed back, increasing the distance between their bodies just enough to slide her hand up his belly, pushing the cotton material as she explored.

His skin burned under her touch, and the beat of his heart pulsed beneath her fingers, its tempo matching her own. When her fingers reached his scar, he reached down, closing his hand over hers. His fingers, warm and strong, pressed down until her hand was flat against his skin, the scar hard under the soft flesh of her palm.

"You've wanted this," he whispered.

"What? To touch your scar?"

"No. This." He crooked his finger under her chin and tilted her head. In one bold movement, he closed his mouth over hers even as his hand dipped farther under her waistband. She gasped as his warm fingers caressed the soft skin of her rear. His fingers tensed, kneading her tender flesh, the sensation sending chills through her body despite the warmth of his skin against hers.

With slow, purposeful movements, he eased his fingers lower, his hand curving under her even as she tried to stay perfectly still, afraid that even the slightest movement would startle him from his purpose. He teased her, his fingers dancing over her soft folds but never quite possessing her, until she whimpered, the simple noise begging him to stop the torment.

He must have understood, because his finger dipped inside her. Such a simple touch, but it sent rocket waves of pleasure crashing through her. She tried to analyze the situation, but she couldn't. Her brain wasn't functioning. She could only feel, could only re-act from some deep primal place inside her. Closing her eyes, she shifted her weight, moving her feet apart and giving him better access to her body, frustrated when his fingers didn't immediately move to stroke and caress her.

She uttered a tiny moan, and he leaned forward to nibble on her earlobe even as he whispered for her to be patient. His breath tickled her cheek, and she tilted her head back, opening her eyes just long enough to see the passion reflected on his face. He wanted this, too, and she relished the surge of feminine power that flowed through her.

She pressed against him, her body quivering when she felt the hard length of him against her thigh. She praised and cursed their clothes, both thankful and frustrated that the barrier was there to keep her from taking this too far.

His caresses were like fire, and she knew he wanted her just as much as she wanted him. At least, his body did. Whether or not the thinking part of Carter wanted her was a question to which she still didn't know the answer. And, until she was sure what he wanted, she didn't intend to compromise her position.

"Tori." His whisper danced on the air, tickling her senses. Her name on his lips was somehow more erotic than his hands on her body. She trembled, uncomfortable with the way her thoughts were heading, even more with the way her body was reacting.

She wanted him, yes, but not at the cost of control.

Calling on every ounce of strength in her body, she pulled away, not looking at him until they were no longer touching and she knew she wouldn't give in and rush back into the comfort of his arms.

Taking a deep breath, she looked up, her eyes meeting his. His eyes were still warm, but she saw confusion there. She stood a little straighter, silently reminding herself that she was doing the right thing. It wouldn't impact her career anymore; she knew that. Agents dated all the time, and the damage from their rendezvous at Quantico had already been done. But even so, taking this further would be a mistake. She knew it, and surely so did Carter.

Which meant that if she didn't pull away, he would. And she refused to be the one left hanging.

Holding her head high, she flashed him a smile. "You see? I told you."

He frowned. "Told me?"

"We don't need the sex."

"Sweetheart, we may not need it, but I think I can safely say we both damn sure wanted it."

"Can you?" She opened her eyes wide, her expression designed to convey maximum surprise. "Not to burst your bubble, Sinclair, but I just wanted to prove my point." It was a lie, of course, and she paused for a moment, half afraid lightning would strike her down. But the lie was for the best, because if she told the truth, he'd know she was truly attracted to him. And that would mean she'd be playing from a position of weakness. And that was unacceptable.

His jaw hardened. "Your point?" He half-snorted, the noise raw and angry. "Why the hell am I not surprised? This is your modus operandi, after all. Start, then stop, just to get your own way. Just to prove some damned point or just to win some damned competition."

She crossed her arms over her chest. "Well, I was right." She lifted her chin. "I wanted to prove that we can play the loving, sensual couple without actually doing the wild thing. And I think I proved that just fine."

His eyes flashed. He was angry, and she couldn't really blame him. But she'd taken control, and right then, that was what mattered.

Suddenly, his hand closed over hers, his fingers like a vise. "I'm not so sure," he said, his voice low.

She licked her lips, put off by something in his tone. "No? About what?"

"I'm not so sure you were right," he said.

She tried to laugh, but it came out more a nervous giggle. "Oh, please. You saw how we were. Two people who can pretend to be that hot for each other should be able to fool the experts at the Kama Resort."

"I'm not saying we'll have any trouble at the resort," he said.

He reached up and brushed a lock of hair off her cheek, hooking it behind her ear. She shivered from the touch, wanting nothing more than to turn tail and run to the B and B. But she stood her ground, her chin high as she looked him in the eye. "Then what are you saying?"

"That it wasn't fake," he said, his voice holding an edge of anger. "That it wasn't just an act."

She swallowed, her gaze moving from his eyes to his chin. "Of course it was."

His thumb and forefinger caught her by the chin, tugging her forward even as he bent toward her. She gasped, but swallowed the sound as his lips closed over hers, hard and demanding. The kiss ended before it had even begun, and she stood there trembling, her eyes half-open as he pulled away.

"I don't think so," Carter said. "And for the record, sweetheart, I intend to prove you wrong."

8

CARTER TIGHTENED his hands around the wooden railing of the deck overlooking the beach. They were at the B and B, and Tori had gone to the room while Carter had chosen to pour himself a scotch. Or two. Or three. He stood staring toward the sea with his drink in his hand, trying to untangle the mishmash of emotions raging through him.

He was a fool. A damn fool. He might as well plaster a big red F on his forehead, because he sure as hell had managed to step off the deep end with Tori.

With a sigh, he slammed back the last of his drink, the potent liquid burning down his throat. He leaned forward, letting the heat of the alcohol overtake the heat of desire.

He'd been an idiot. Instead of using his brain, he'd been led astray by other parts of his body. Parts that seemed out of control where Tori was concerned.

With Tori, though, it was easy to lose control. She had a spark about her—an energy—that he tried to resist. But somehow he was drawn to it like a moth to a flame. Considering how often the poor stupid bugs burned to death, he wasn't at all sure he liked the analogy. But there it was. He'd been attracted to her at the academy, and that attraction hadn't faded in the past few years even though he knew better.

If anything, she'd become more alluring. She still

had that competitive edge, but somehow she'd become softer even while becoming harder. Softer because she was willing to talk and joke with him, whereas before she would only say the minimum necessary to satisfy whatever assignment they'd shared. Harder because her confidence had increased. She might have been holed up in a cubicle, but it hadn't damaged her ego. Tori knew what she wanted and was more than willing to chase after her dream even if that meant stepping on a few poor slobs like Carter. The dichotomy was odd, but undeniably appealing.

He supposed that in some ways they were alike. He was chasing after his dream, too. This job meant everything. And that meant he wasn't about to let Tori screw it up for him. The question, of course, was how to keep a handle on her.

He knew she wanted their mission to succeed just as he did, so he didn't think she'd intentionally screw it up. But she was overeager and inexperienced in undercover work. Couple that with the fact that she was jealous of his position as team leader, and he was faced with a recipe for disaster. And he needed to figure out a way to rein in a woman who made the blood boil in his veins but who absolutely, positively didn't want to submit to him.

Before tonight, his attraction to Tori had been a glowing ember. Tonight, it had turned into a raging inferno. And the hell of it was, Tori had lost control just as much as he had. Maybe Quantico had been an act and maybe it hadn't, but he knew for damn sure that her reaction to him tonight hadn't been fake. She'd been just as turned on as Carter. Only she wouldn't admit it. So not only was he left to suffer under the remnants of one hell of a hard-on, but he was also suffering at the hands of a smug partner who seemed to think that she'd got the better of him.

Well, he supposed she had.

Damn Tori and her ridiculous competitiveness. If she hadn't pulled back, they could have gone to their room and made love all night. His stomach clenched as he considered the possibility of losing himself to her throughout the night.

Not the best way to run an operation, of course, but with Tori, the traditional rules didn't apply. If they'd made love—if they'd got it out of their system—they'd be on an even footing when they went onto the resort.

Apparently, though, Tori wasn't too keen on the even-footing plan. She wasn't hard to read; he'd give her that. He'd figured out easily enough that to Tori, even their attraction was a competition.

He picked up his drink, swirling the ice in the otherwise empty glass as his mind focused on Tori. By pulling away, she could hold onto some illusion of power in their relationship. With any other woman, he might let her hold onto that illusion. But with Tori...well, with Tori that would be dangerous.

He tossed back the glass, sucking in some ice, then bit down on the cube, the cold against his teeth making inroads against the fuzz in his brain. In truth, she'd left him with only one choice. If he wanted to maintain control of this mission, he was going to have to seduce her. He smiled to himself. After Quantico, *that* was an assignment he was more than looking forward to.

ALONE IN THE ROOM, Tori paced. Back and forth, back and forth, until she was pretty sure she was going to have to reimburse Phyllis for the worn spot on the carpet.

It simply wasn't fair. She balled her fists as she made another pass across the room. She'd stuck to her guns, tamped down on her desire, and still she was frustrated as hell.

Walking away from Carter hadn't been a mistake, but it sure as hell felt like one.

Stifling a groan, she shoved her hands deep in the pockets of her shorts and fell face first onto the soft mattress. She'd won. No doubt about it, she'd taken the upper hand in this little game they'd been playing, and she'd won the grand prize.

Too bad it was only a Pyrrhic victory. She may have won, but she was also alone in their shared bedroom, her body still warm and tingly from his touch and with absolutely no prospects of satisfying a certain itch that only Carter could scratch.

So much for the best laid plans.

Sighing, she hugged herself tight. The fact was, Carter had left her damn frustrated. No, *she'd* left herself frustrated. After all, she'd been the one who'd walked away.

And she'd do it again if she had to. Despite the very serious downside of a very serious lust that longed to be satisfied, she'd grabbed hold and exercised a moment of control. And in doing so, she'd avoided the risk of being humiliated if he put on the brakes.

She nibbled on her lower lip. Of course, there really was no reason she had to sit here in the room all hot and bothered. She was a modern girl. Carter might have worked her up, getting her to a point where she was craving a primal release. But Carter wasn't there anymore, and there was certainly no rule saying she couldn't finish the job herself.

She glanced at the door. He had a key, and there

wasn't any chain, so there was no way to keep him out. But he'd been more than a little miffed after they'd trudged to the room in silence. He'd immediately headed for the living room and the wet bar. Considering how irritated he'd been, she doubted he'd be joining her anytime soon. For that matter, she might find him on the living room couch in the morning, with Phyllis bent over him handing out relationship advice.

She half-snorted. A relationship between her and Carter. The concept really was funny. Even funnier since they had to pretend to be madly in love. Or, at least, madly in lust.

Love might be hard. She didn't love him, and she wasn't interested at this point in her life with falling in love with anybody. But lust? Well, the one thing that made this assignment a walk in the park was that she didn't have to fake the lust angle.

Even now, her body still tingled, and it had been over an hour since their escapade on the beach. Crossing her arms, she slipped her hands under her unbuttoned shirt, her fingers caressing her shoulders. With one quick move, she pushed the shirt off, letting it fall to the floor. The window in the room was open, and the cool ocean breeze caressed her bare skin until she wasn't sure if the goose bumps on her arm were the result of the night air or her decadent thoughts about Carter.

Not that it mattered. At the moment, all that mattered was getting him out of her system. She couldn't admit to him how much he'd affected her, but right then she was all alone. Nothing was holding her back, and she intended to find the release she couldn't take on the beach.

Determined, she untied the knot between her shoulder blades, then pushed her hair away to unfasten the knot at the base of her neck. Taking a deep breath, she let the bikini top fall away, her hands following its path as it fell over her breasts to the ground.

Her palms caressed her nipples, and her breasts tightened, warm with the heat of desire. She gasped, surprised by the power of her reaction to such a simple touch. Arching her back, she traced her fingers down her belly, stopping at the waistband of her shorts. Closing her eyes, she slipped her hand under, imagining it was Carter's fingers that were caressing her, sliding over the smooth material of her swimsuit bottom.

She dipped lower, her finger tracing the edge of the material at the soft spot of her inner thigh. A tremble raked her body, and she held on to the bedpost with her free hand. The thinking part of her mind urged her to stop, but the rest of her wanted release. The rest of her wanted Carter and, barring that, she wanted the fantasy of Carter.

Decided, she slipped her hand out, mourning the lost touch, and unfastened her shorts. With both hands, she pushed the material down, and her bikini bottom along with it.

She stood there, naked in their room, as the evening breeze caressed her. With her eyes closed, she imagined it was Carter's gentle touch moving so sweetly over her body, and she added her own touch to the fantasy, stroking herself as she wanted him to stroke her.

With a light touch, she skimmed her side, under her arm and beside her breast. Barely a whisper of a touch, the pressure of her fingertips on the sensitive skin still made her body come alive.

Moaning, she moved to the bed, then traced her hand lower, teasing herself by drawing circles on her belly. Lower and lower she moved her fingers, teasing but never quite satisfying. With her eyes closed, she imagined Carter walking into the room and seeing her there. Totally cool, she'd show no embarrassment at all. She'd just spread her legs wider in silent invitation.

His eyes would darken, but otherwise he wouldn't react. Not until he pulled off his shirt, one bold movement that would leave her gasping in anticipation. He'd take off his shorts next, along with his swimsuit, and he'd already be aroused. He'd walk to her without saying a word, and she'd have to fight not to cry out and beg him to hurry.

When he reached the bed, he'd straddle her, and the length of his desire would press hard against her belly. But he wouldn't enter her. Instead, he'd lower his mouth to hers and kiss her, deep and wet, even as his hands stroked her shoulders.

Nibbling on her lower lip, he'd ease his hands down and stroke her breasts. With her eyes closed, she imagined his touch as he moved down her body, and with her own hands, she stroked and teased her breasts until her nipples were so tight they were almost painful. In her mind, his hands moved down her body, his fingertips rough against her skin. She mimicked his movements, the path of her fingers leaving a trail of fire along her body.

She knew he wasn't there, knew she was alone in the room, but still her body sizzled and throbbed, delighting in Carter's touch, in Carter's sensuous teases. In his little nips and kisses. In the way his fingers teased and his lips tormented.

With a low moan, she pulled one hand to her mouth, sucking on her thumb even as she imagined taking one of Carter's fingers between her lips and tormenting him with her tongue. With her other hand, she skimmed downward, imagining Carter's mouth dancing over her skin as he moved lower and lower.

A hard tremble shook her body, and she reached down, letting her fingers—letting *Carter*—explore her most intimate places. Warm and wet, her body opened to his sensuous exploration.

Keeping her eyes closed, she imagined his breath hot against her, his tongue teasing her, finding her most sensitive point and then stroking, sucking, tormenting until...

Until...

No.

With a gasp, she pulled her hand away, forcing herself to sit up. Her body might want the climax, but her mind refused to give in to Carter. And even though he wasn't there—wasn't really in the room—if she lost herself to his imaginary touch, somehow he'd win all the same. Even if she'd be the only one who knew it.

Groaning, she pulled herself off the bed and headed for the bathroom, gathering things along the way. She rarely resorted to cold showers, but right now she definitely needed one.

Leaving her clothes on the floor, she padded to the bathroom and turned on the water. The temptation to take a long, hot shower tugged at her, but she was determined to take a cold one first. She might have some sand between her toes, but this shower wasn't for the purpose of getting her clean. She needed to get a certain man off her mind, and a steamy, soapy shower simply wasn't the ticket.

Phyllis's place had no problems with water pressure, and the cold spray hammered the shower floor. Even from beyond the tub, the mist chilled her, and her resolve weakened. Maybe she'd start out warm and slowly...*very* slowly...she'd shift the temperature to cold. Same result, less shock to the system.

That made sense, and she adjusted the water to a nice, soothing temperature. She stepped in, tightly closing the opaque shower curtain so she wouldn't accidentally flood the bathroom.

The water was as hot as she could stand it, and billows of steam filled the area enclosed by the curtain. She breathed in deep, letting the warm mist relax her even as the pulsating hot water went to work on her muscles. The sheen of desire might not be fading, but she had to admit a long hot shower felt awfully good.

The bathroom was well-stocked for honeymooners, and she took a loofah from a basket and drenched it with berry-scented bath gel. With her back to the curtain, she propped her leg on the side of the tub, bending slightly at the waist so she could lean over and rub the sponge over her leg.

A soft click caught her attention, and she stood up, her head cocked as she tried to pinpoint the source of the sound. "Carter?"

No answer.

She frowned, wondering if he'd come into the room and was ignoring her. Pulling the curtain aside, she listened more intently, but the sound wasn't repeated. After a quick glance to make sure her gun was still on the counter within reaching distance, she went back to her shower, concentrating on the other leg. Probably nothing. After all, it was an old house, and old houses were filled with creaks and groans and unusual noises.

The mist from the shower swirled around her, and as she concentrated on her leg, the spray pounded on her back. She knew she should turn down the heat and add some cold to the water, but she wasn't quite ready to let go of the sensual warmth that had crept over her. Besides, she wasn't thinking about Carter. Well, not much.

"It's like a rain forest in here."

Her pulse quickened as Carter's voice filtered toward her through the mist.

She cried out, straightening and dropping the loofah. In one motion, she turned to face the still-closed shower curtain. She saw his shadow as he moved about the bathroom. It loomed larger, a sign that he was approaching.

"What do you think you're doing in here?" she asked, trying to keep her voice firm, but afraid it was squeaking.

"What do I think I'm doing? Babe, I'm doing exactly what you think I am."

"Being an asshole?"

He laughed, and his shadow moved closer.

Frantic, she looked around for something to cover herself with, but found nothing more substantial than the loofah. She bent over to pick it up and positioned it over the apex of her thighs, her other arm crossed over her breasts.

The shadow loomed closer, and she held her breath. She knew she should be screaming for him to get out of there, but for some reason, she couldn't speak. Instead, she just watched, her eyes wide, as his fingers curled around the curtain. Slowly, he pulled it aside, the rings clacking against the shower rod as he methodically pulled the curtain back.

A nervous laugh escaped her, sounding hollow to her ears, and she took a step backward until her back was pressed against the tile wall. The cool of the tile in contrast to the heat of her body fortified her nerve, and she stood straighter, still keeping her loofah and her arm properly positioned. "What the hell are you doing here?"

"Isn't it obvious?"

"That you've lost your mind? Yes. It is obvious." She nodded toward the towel rack. "If you'll just pass me one of those towels, I'll get out of here and we can forget this ever happened."

"I don't think so."

She raised an eyebrow, trying for haughty, which wasn't easy considering the circumstances. "Excuse me?"

"I'm here to finish what we started." His gaze raked over her body, starting at her head and working down to her toes. The heat from the shower surrounded her, but that was nothing compared to the heat he was generating with nothing more than a look. "Today, and back at Quantico."

She swallowed and tried to take a step backward. Not possible, of course, since there was a wall blocking her path. Mentally, she dug her heels in, telling herself that she didn't want this. Whatever he'd come to offer, she didn't want it.

But that was a big, fat, hairy lie, and she knew that if he pressed her on the point, she'd sleep with him. She wanted to as much as she didn't want to, and in the end, desire would win.

Too bad for her, she'd end up hating herself for it. He'd win, and once again she'd be second place to Carter Sinclair.

Taking a deep breath, she looked him in the eye. "I'd appreciate it if you'd leave."

"Sorry, Lowell. Not gonna happen." He lifted his

foot and stepped into the tub, still clad in his shorts and T-shirt.

"What the devil are you doing?"

"Right now I'm getting in the shower with you. In a minute, though, I'm planning on seducing you."

"Oh." Not exactly the best response, but under the circumstances it was all she could come up with. "Seducing me?"

"Yes, ma'am." He leaned forward, resting his hands on the tile wall and trapping her in the circle of his arms. "I figure I got gypped on the beach. And I know I got gypped at the academy. I figure it's time to even the score."

Oh my. She fought the temptation to move the few inches toward him and capture his mouth with her own. *No.* She needed to fight this. Needed to get him out of there. And then she needed to switch the faucet all the way to cold and freeze these wanton feelings right out of her.

"Agent," she said, trying to lace her voice with a touch of authority, "this is totally inappropriate behavior. Please leave now before I have to take action that we'll both regret."

His eyes darkened, and she knew she'd struck a nerve. "All right," he said. He dropped his hands, releasing her from the prison of his arms. "Tell me to go and I'll go."

She licked her lips. "I already told you to go."

"No," he said. "Tell me *now.* Now that I've told you why I'm here. Now that we both know what I want. Tell me to go. Say it out loud, and I'm out of here." He hooked a finger under her chin and tilted her head. "I'll head out that door and we'll both forget this ever

happened and get back to our assignment like good little agents. All you have to do is say the word."

Except she couldn't say it. She tried. She really did.
She opened her mouth, fully expecting that she'd
calmly and clearly tell him to leave the bathroom. To
leave her alone and never try to tempt her again.

But when she spoke, all she said was, "You've been
drinking."

"Actually, babe, I have." He grinned, slow and
smug, and she knew that he understood. She'd backed
down. She'd opened the door. And, damn her, in doing
so she'd lost ground.

"But I'm a long way from drunk," he said. "Only
bold."

"Bold?" She swallowed, half afraid she was tempting fate by asking, and half afraid she wasn't.

"Bold enough to do this." His arm slipped around
her waist, and he pulled her close. The loofah ended up
pressed tight between them, and he shifted against it,
his chuckle soft against her ear. "Hang on to that,
sweetheart. Maybe later we can find an interesting use
for it."

"I can think of a few," she said. She heard her voice,
soft and sultry, and the sound pulled her to reality.
Closing her eyes, she backed away. "I...I'm sorry. I
can't do this. I do want to, but I can't."

He pulled the T-shirt over his head. "Yes, babe, you
can." He dropped the shirt, soaked, to the floor of the
tub. "Sex camp, remember? Intimacy. Young lovers
with an amazing sex life looking to spice it up."

"I think I already proved that we can fake it just
fine."

He unbuttoned his shorts, then started to tug at the
zipper. "Is that what you do? Fake it?"

She bit back a smile, determined not to give in. "I've faked it once or twice."

"Not with me, you haven't." The shorts came off, dropping to the bottom of the tub with a wet splat.

She licked her lips. "Of course not, since we've never done anything."

"No thanks to you," he said, a hard edge to his voice.

"What's that supposed to mean?"

"Just that everything to you is a competition—a way to prove a point. Earlier tonight, and back at Quantico."

"A competition? We were on a date," she said. She knelt to retrieve his shirt, pressing it against her breasts and belly.

"Cut the crap, Lowell. You went out with me at the academy because you wanted to blow my concentration. And you ran away for the same reason."

She shifted backward, pressing against the tiles. "You're nuts. I went out with you because I thought you were hot. And I ran away because that guy was staring at us." She licked her lips. "And then, after my head cleared..." She trailed off with a shrug. "Well, we'd been on the verge of making a mistake anyway. So it was just as well I left."

"You thought I was hot?"

She arched a brow. "I was young and foolish."

He ignored the sarcasm, his brow furrowing. "So there wasn't a ploy? No plan to try and blow my concentration so you could slide into my slot?"

She tilted her head, oddly flattered by the thought that being seduced by her would be enough to blow his concentration. And when she looked at him, it was with a smile. "Believe me, Sinclair. I could beat you—

hell, I *can* beat you. And I don't have to resort to seduction to do it."

"But you didn't beat me," he said.

"Yet," she said. She met his eye. "Everything is a competition to me. Remember? You said it yourself."

He laughed. "Okay. I guess we're back where we started." He reached out and peeled his wet shirt off her body. "Babe, you haven't faked it with me."

The bulge evident under his swimsuit made perfectly clear that he was willing to correct that little oversight right then, right there. She managed to pull her gaze to his face. "Is that a challenge?"

He shook his head. "No. I never bet where women faking orgasms is concerned." His grin totally disarmed her. "Bad karma, you know."

"Oh." Too bad. She was looking for a reason, any reason, to give in to him. Proving to him that she could fake an orgasm without him knowing the difference... Okay, it wasn't the best excuse, but at the moment she didn't need the best. Any old excuse would do.

"Stamina, though..." A wicked grin played on the corner of his lips.

"What?"

"Well, a young couple that's supposed to be as hot as we're pretending..." He shrugged. "The folks at the resort are going to figure we're going at it like bunnies."

She crossed her arms over her chest. "Unless this resort is more avant garde than I thought, no one's going to know what we do behind closed doors."

"True." He stroked her cheek. "But I do so much better undercover when I really live the part. Don't you?"

She swallowed. "This is my first undercover assignment, remember?"

"Then you should trust me on this," he said. He gave her a sideways look. "But that's okay. You probably haven't worked out much since the academy. If you're afraid you can't keep up with me..."

She should call his bluff and turn him down flat. But she wanted him, too. She licked her lips, trying to decide what to do. Finally, she dropped the loofah and took a step toward him. Without ever taking her eyes from his face, she put her hands on his hips just above the elastic waist of his swimsuit. "Well, I suppose if method acting is the key to a successful undercover assignment...who am I to try a different tack?"

CARTER MOANED as Tori pressed her lips to his. And when her hands slid down, taking the wet material of his swimsuit with them, he thought he might explode right then, right there. He'd come to the room to seduce her, to even the score and, yes, to get even with her for using him years ago.

Only it turned out she hadn't used him. She'd left, true, but not for the reasons he'd thought. And he was naked in the shower with this woman, and suddenly he wanted her even more. What had started as lust born of anger was turning into something else. Still lust, true. He wasn't in love with Tori; he couldn't be. But it was a lust tinged with respect. She was as competitive as hell, but she was also smart enough to know that she was competitive as hell.

Still, she'd regretted their tryst at Quantico, that much was clear, and he needed to know she wouldn't regret tonight. He cupped her cheeks and pulled away, his eyes boring into hers. "Are you sure?" he whispered.

"I'm sure," she said. She flashed him a cocky grin. "I've always wanted to try method acting."

"Well, then," he said, pressing close, "here's hoping we both break a leg."

He slid his hands along her back, cupping her rear as he urged her closer. She moaned, but her body stiffened, and he immediately backed off.

"Tori?"

"No," she whispered. "Don't stop. I was just thinking that we're going to break more than a leg if we don't get out of this slick tub and into a warm bed." She tried to move past him, but his arm was still around her waist, and he pulled her back.

"Not so fast. I have plans for this shower." He pushed a strand of hair behind her ear, imagining all the decadent possibilities.

"Plans?"

"Unless you think you could do a better job planning our little tête-à-tête?"

She laughed. "I'm pretty sure I can do anything you can do...and I can do it better."

He gasped as she held onto the handrail and lifted her foot, tracing the curve of his calf with her instep. The touch, somehow more erotic than losing himself inside her, set his blood boiling.

"But since I don't know what you have in mind, I don't know what I have to beat. So you just go right ahead. And maybe later I'll show you what real planning can accomplish."

Her mouth twitched, and he knew she was holding back a smile. Hell, so was he. If anyone had told Tori at the academy that one day she'd be using the intense competition between them as an excuse to have sex with him, Carter imagined she probably would have pulled out her gun and shot them.

Now, though, she seemed perfectly happy to have the excuse. And he was certainly happy to have given it to her.

"Turn around," he said. "And, agent, you can consider that an order."

WITH A MOCK SALUTE, Tori complied, and when she was facing the light blue tiles of the shower wall, he pressed behind her, molding her body to his from his chest to his knees. She stifled a sigh. There was something unbelievably erotic about a man who knew her so well he could tap into her competitiveness as a means for seduction. Erotic, and a little unnerving.

Not that she intended to question his methods. Not then, anyway. Right then, all she wanted was to lose herself in his touch. To let him satisfy her the way she'd been unwilling to satisfy herself.

He reached beside her and pressed some gel from the wall dispenser into his hand. From behind her, she could hear him rubbing his palms together, then his hands closed over her shoulders as he rubbed the lather down her arms. When his hands reached hers, he massaged each of her fingers. Hardly an erogenous zone, but considering the effect his touch was having on her, he might as well have been massaging her G-spot.

Tilting her head, she moaned low in the back of her throat.

"You like that?"

"I take the Fifth," she said.

His lips grazed up the back of her neck, the deep sound of his chuckle tickling her senses. "Now, see?

That's the beauty of my job. I know that when you take the Fifth you're hiding something. Like maybe you're hiding that the answer is yes."

She tried to think of a comeback but couldn't quite get her mind in gear. Carter didn't seem to mind her silence. Taking her hands, he pressed them to the tile with a whisper. "Stay just like that."

Somehow, she managed a whimper of consent. Around them, the spray from the shower pulsed, surrounding them with a liquid heat that didn't even begin to match the wet heat flowing through her veins and pooling between her thighs.

"Please," she whispered, turning at the waist. She wanted to face him, wanted to have some semblance of control, but Carter wasn't about to let her.

"Patience, grasshopper." With his hands firmly on her hips, he turned her face to the tile. "No peeking. I want you just to feel." His hands raked up her body, his fingers cupping her breasts and teasing her hard nipples until she thought she would cry out from the pleasure of his touch.

When he pulled away, she bit her lip to keep from crying in frustration. She heard a metallic clicking, then the pulse of the shower seemed to change in tempo. With a start, she realized he'd removed the handheld showerhead.

Tori had never considered herself the most imaginative person on the planet, but she didn't have any trouble at all imagining what he intended to do with that pulsating stream of water. Her body stiffened in anticipation, and without thinking, she spread her legs, shifting them apart on the slick shower floor even as she tried to find better footing.

Carter grazed the back of her neck with kisses. "So you think you know what I've got planned for you?"

"Y-yes." She had to work to control her voice.

"I think you're probably right," he whispered, the smile in his voice coming through loud and clear. As he spoke, she felt the pulse from the showerhead on the back of her calf. The water beating against her, combined with the way Carter stroked her side with his free hand, took her right to the edge.

Her fingers flexed, trying to find a better purchase on the slick tile wall. She was afraid that, when he finally brought her to climax, she'd buckle and collapse in a heap on the shower floor. She didn't have long to worry about that, though. Carter's actions soon took her mind off anything except the exquisite feel of his touch—and the touch of the warm water—against her flesh.

The erotic pulse of water inched up the back of her thigh, a few stray droplets tickling and teasing that secret area between her thighs. Carter's free hand traced a path upward, his thumb finally stopping at her mouth. He traced the outline of her lip as she gasped, frantically shifting her hips in an effort to will that elusive spray of water where she truly wanted it.

But Carter kept tormenting her. He played the water up the back of her thigh, almost but not quite aiming the pulsating spray between her thighs. She whimpered, frustrated, and he slipped his forefinger into her mouth. Closing her eyes, she drew his finger in, sucking and teasing, trying to arouse him as he'd aroused her. Hoping he'd take her right there and end the sweet torment.

His groan told her she wasn't alone in her frustration. She played her tongue over his rough skin, her lips tightening around his finger as she drew him in over and over. Behind her, Carter pressed close, his body aligned with hers. His erection pressed against her, and fire shot through her body. Her knees were like jelly, and if he weren't pressed against her, holding her upright, she knew she would glide to the floor in a boneless mass of goo.

His hips rocked against hers in an erotic rhythm that set ever cell in her body spinning. The steam from the shower filled her throat, covering them in a fine mist.

"We're going to run out of hot water soon," she said when he slipped his finger from her mouth.

"Don't worry," he said, moving his hand downward to caress her neck. "I'm almost through with you."

She almost sagged with relief at his words. But even in her relief lurked disappointment. Did he mean *through* as in finished? Because right then, nothing sounded less appealing than the possibility of losing Carter's touch.

She didn't have time to worry about his meaning, though. With obvious purpose, he slipped his hand down, once again teasing her nipple between thumb and forefinger. She bit back a gasp only to find that same gasp escape when he moved the pulsating showerhead forward, aiming it at the apex of her thighs.

"Spread your legs," he whispered.

She shook her head. "I can't." She was too on edge. The stream of water was too much, too intense, and she truly didn't think she could handle what he had in mind for her.

"Yes, you can." Even as he spoke, he was turning her around, urging her to face him. He gave her one quick kiss before he began trailing his lips downward. Her chin. Her neck. Her collarbone.

Then lower still, his lips caressing the soft curve of her breast, then moving down, lower and lower, to her belly button. His free hand followed, first holding her waist, then her right hip, as he steadied himself for his downward progression. His goal seemed pretty apparent, and Tori held her breath, silently urging him on.

With one hand, he still wielded the torment of that showerhead, and he adjusted the stream to a less powerful pulse. The water spewed against her thigh, the warmth making her even wetter, a condition that had nothing to do with the fact that she was standing in a shower.

When he aimed the water between her legs, she cried out. The pulse tickled and teased, but only danced around the edges of satisfaction. She needed more, and she writhed against the water, trying to find release but unable to catch its fleeting edges.

"Shh." With his mouth pressed against her belly, she felt his whisper more than heard it. "Trust me."

Lower and lower, his mouth moved, his tongue tracing patterns on her flesh. She reached out, grabbing the handrail to steady herself as her body quaked and quivered.

With his tongue, he traced the soft inner fold of her thigh as she tried not to melt underneath him. When the ministrations of his tongue were joined by the pulse of warm water, Tori was certain her body was going to explode if he didn't soon take her all the way.

"Please," she whispered.

"Please what?" he murmured, his breath stroking her intimately.

"Touch me," she said. She wanted to yell, to scream for him to make her come, but somehow an uncharacteristic shyness overcame her, and she could only hope he understood her unspoken request.

Of course, he did.

"Like this?" he asked, then dipped his tongue lower, finding her most sensitive spot.

She couldn't answer. Could only nod even though he certainly couldn't see her affirmative response.

He must have understood, though, because he certainly didn't waste any time in fulfilling her most ardent desires. With his tongue, he laved her center, already hot and slick from both the shower and her desire. The steady pulse of the shower accompanied the intimate kisses, pleasure building and building until she was sure she would collapse unless he stopped.

Arching her back, she tried to draw away even as she tried to concentrate on the sensations, to focus and center them. He dropped the showerhead, his hands going to cup her rear and steady her even as he pulled her closer.

Relentless.

Her entire body was on fire, and yet he did nothing to cool her down, instead pouring fuel on the already burning embers. "Carter," she cried as the pressure built and built. "Please."

And with that one simple word, he took her. His mouth finding her center and pushing her to heights of pure pleasure. She reached down, her fingers intertwined in his hair as she rocked against him, losing herself to the power of the moment.

"Oh, God," she whispered, rubbing the back of her hand over her mouth as the moment faded and the world settled on its axis.

He slid up her, their bodies gliding together as if they were oiled. "Tell me what you want," he said, his voice low and husky against her ear. "Do you want me to stop now? Or do you want more?"

She breathed in deep, her body still trembling from the force of her orgasm. Even if they weren't competing—even if she didn't intend to show him that her stamina could match his orgasm for orgasm—there was only one answer to that question. "More," she whispered. "Please, Carter. I want more."

9

THE WOMAN in his arms was driving him insane.

Carter wasn't sure what he'd expected when he set out to seduce Tori, but it certainly wasn't the hot, responsive woman in his arms. Never once had he seen Tori lose control.

Never once, that is, until now.

She'd lost control, all right. And she'd lost it with him. The knowledge both thrilled and humbled him.

He'd watched her face after she found her release and was absolutely certain he'd never before seen anything as beautiful in his life. When he'd stood up, he'd gathered her in his arms, pressing against her and holding her close until her heartbeat calmed and her breathing returned to normal. He stroked her hair, wet and silky from the shower, as she snuggled against him, her chin on his shoulder.

"Wow," she whispered.

He kissed the top of her head. "You could say that."

"I did say that."

He laughed, surprised once again by her playfulness. He didn't know this Tori, not really, but he was damn sure looking forward to making her acquaintance.

With one arm still tight around her shoulders, he reached over and pulled the shower curtain aside, glancing at the small clock on the counter next to the sink. "So what do you think?" he asked, a tease in his voice. "Are you sure you want more? Maybe a little break is in order? Some dessert? A midnight snack."

Her eyes widened, and she poked him in the chest with the tip of her finger. "A break? What are you, a wimp?"

"Nope. Just trying to be chivalrous and offer you a bite to eat."

She licked her lips. "More like you're trying to be devious and get me to quit before you do."

"I take the Fifth," he said, stealing her earlier excuse.

"Uh-huh. Well, I'm not hungry." She licked her lips. "Not for anything from Phyllis's kitchen, anyway."

"Oh, really?"

She cocked an eyebrow. "Unless you're weak from hunger." She traced her finger down the edge of his jaw, her smooth skin scraping against his evening beard. "If that's the case, this was the easiest victory I've ever claimed."

"Believe me, sweetheart, you haven't won yet."

"No? Then take me into that bedroom and prove it." She grinned. "There's a box of condoms in my overnight bag. Maybe the bet should be whether or not we can use them all up."

"Sounds like a bet to me," he said. Leaning over, he caught her under the legs and scooped her up, managing to get them into the bedroom without stumbling and killing them both.

"I'm impressed," she said. "Guess it wasn't a fluke when you aced the physical training section at the academy."

Her voice was casual, but he knew his success still irked her. Wanting to keep the moment light, he laid her on the bed and straddled her. "I had no choice but to beat you," he said as she writhed beneath him. "If I was behind you, I'd be staring at your ass all day and wouldn't accomplish anything." He waggled his eyebrows. "It's one fine rear end you've got there."

"You're a goof," she said.

"Maybe," he agreed. "But I do like your ass."

Her cheek flushed pink under his steady gaze, and Carter gave himself a brownie point for rendering Tori speechless. "You're blushing," he said.

"I don't blush."

He hid a smile. "Whatever you say." He kissed the tip of her nose, then traced his lips over her cheek to finally settle lightly on her mouth. "I guess you must just be sunburned," he murmured.

Her arms snaked around his neck, pulling him closer. "Guess so. Because I don't blush."

"You're sure? Because—"

But he couldn't finish the thought. Her lips clamped onto his, her tongue seeking entrance to his mouth as her hands stroked his back. Fire whipped through his body, and he groaned as he fought the desire to press her against the bed and sink into her.

"My turn to take the lead. Okay, boss man? Or are you the team leader for every aspect of this little adventure?"

"I think we can make an exception for you, Lowell," he said, intrigued by the idea of Tori taking the lead sexually. "From now until sunrise, you can call the shots."

"Yeah? Good."

Before Carter knew it, she flipped them over. She was straddling him, her naked thighs pressed against his waist even as her soft rear rubbed him, teasing his oh-so-hard erection.

"Let me guess," he said, eyeing the enticing view just above his navel. "You're planning to torment me all night."

She laughed. "Don't I wish?" Bending at the waist, she eased forward, her breasts stroking his chest as her lips caressed his cheek, then his ear. He closed his eyes, losing himself to the sensation of her skin against his. "Unfortunately," she said, "that would torture me, too, and I'm not into masochism."

"I'll file that away for future reference," he said.

"You do that," she whispered, her tongue still teasing his ear. As she spoke, she twitched that firm little butt of hers, rubbing him just slightly, but more than enough to send him to the edge, but no further. And that, of course, was pure, delicious torture.

His hands twitched, and he fought the urge to reach up, grab her hips and move her to exactly where he wanted her—right on top of him.

"Oh, no, you don't." With a sly smile, she wriggled against him, the friction of their bodies rubbing together driving him insane.

"I don't have that much self-control, Tori," he said through gritted teeth. "Unless you want me to flip you over and have my way with you, I'd suggest moving along."

Her delighted laughter reached him, and he fought for control. Apparently, she thought he was kidding.

She arched her back as she faced the ceiling in a luxurious stretch that had the benefit of giving him a fabulous view of her breasts and her belly. And all the regions below...

He smiled to himself. She may be insisting on being in charge, but that didn't mean he couldn't urge her along. Feeling mildly devious—but absolutely justified—he licked his finger, then reached out with the damp digit to trace the edge of her belly button.

"Ah, ah," she said. "My show, remember?"

"I was hoping for an audience participation performance." He trailed his finger lower, then lower still, until he slipped inside her silky smooth folds.

She moaned, her head thrown back and her hands clutching his legs for balance. "No fair," she whispered, her voice husky.

His finger slid in and out, in and out, and she ground against him, her hips undulating in an erotic motion that had him close to climax. "Feel free to steal the scene, babe. I promise you I won't object."

"No?" She lifted her hips up and back, pulling away from his touch. "I'm more than happy to take over, but only if you promise to be a good boy."

"Moi?" He pointed to himself. "Sweetheart, I'm always good."

"And modest, too, I see."

"Always."

"Mmm." Leaning forward, she kissed him hard on the mouth. "Close your eyes."

He opened his mouth to speak, but she silenced him with a finger over his lips.

"My show, remember? No talking. Just close your eyes and do what I say and maybe, just maybe, I'll show you the time of your life."

Now that was an offer he wasn't about to refuse. Closing his eyes, he let the ambiance of the room settle around him. The electronic buzz of the alarm clock, the distant crash of the ocean's waves upon the shore, the steady drip of the shower they hadn't quite turned off. And Tori. His senses were filled with Tori—her clean, summer smell. The smooth skin of her inner thighs grazing the tender skin above his hips. Her fingers, soft and demanding, stroking his chest.

Her weight shifted, and the sheets rustled. A waft of cool air tickled his cheek, and he shivered. Her mouth, as soft as a feather, grazed over his. He opened his mouth, wanting to taste her fully, but she pulled away, her touch dancing lightly on his lips. When she nipped his lower lip, her teeth playing with his sensitive skin, he cried out, then relaxed to her continued ministrations.

"Do you like that?" she whispered.

"Mmm." He didn't trust his throat to make words, so he tried to make one noise of pure pleasure.

Her hands pressed against his stomach again, but this time her skin was slick and warm. He inhaled, caught the subtle scent of flowers and remembered the lotion he'd found in the bathroom.

"You're going to make me smell like a girl," he said.

"If it bothers you, I'll put you in the bath and wash you off."

Her tone was low and sultry, and his body hardened even more from the thought of being bathed by Tori.

Lower and lower her hands moved, and with every fraction of an inch, his desire increased exponentially. His fingers twitched, fighting the desire to reach up and cup her breast, to stoke her mouth, to let her suckle his finger.

A heat built under her hands as she played him. She lifted her butt so the only part of her touching him was the palms of her hands. He made a small noise of protest and was shocked to realize he'd whimpered.

"Don't worry," she whispered. "I'm not going away."

The promise didn't relax him. On the contrary, a fire of anticipation burned through his body, and he fought the urge to cry out and insist—hell, *order* her to take him right then.

Her hands continued their journey of sweet torment, and Carter knew that even if he were so foolish as to demand she end this amazing torture, she wouldn't do it. He'd given her the controls, and she was relishing every moment. Tori was in charge, and all Carter could think was that she was doing damn fine in the role.

Even if she was driving him crazy.

"Please, babe." He forced the words out past the flurry of energy that was swarming through his body.

"Please what?"

"*Now.* Unless you want to watch a very turned-on man explode."

She laughed. "Actually, I do. But not like that." Another kiss graced his lips. "Patience, Agent Sinclair. Didn't they teach you that at Quantico."

"Guess I failed," he growled.

"No, no. I remember. You did very well."

"And now I'm being punished."

"Action and reaction, Sinclair," she said. He felt her lift up, pushing her body away from his. "Action," she said. And then, before he realized what she was doing, she'd slipped a condom on him and was lowering herself, her slick, wet heat enveloping him. "Reaction," she said.

But he couldn't respond. His body was on fire, moving to a rhythm he wasn't dictating. He thrust against her, his hips rising off the bed as his body took over, seeking release.

They rocked together, the pressure building and building until he couldn't hold back any longer. With a deep, guttural groan, he found release, his body trembling from the explosion. Tori ground against him, crying out with her own release before collapsing, limp, on his chest.

With a sigh, he kissed the top of her head, deeply satisfied when she snuggled closer in response, her fingers drawing idle patterns on his chest. After an eternity of laying together like that, she scooted off, curling next to him and pulling the sheet up to cover them.

When she turned to look at him, he noticed the way her teeth dragged over her lower lip. "How was it for you?" she asked, an uncharacteristic hint of uncertainty in her voice.

He rolled over, pulling her with him until she was cuddled between his chest and his arm. "Sweetheart, that was perfect," he said. And it had been. But even if it hadn't, he would have said so anyway. Right then, all he wanted was to reassure Tori.

He'd told himself she wasn't the type of woman he'd want permanently, but he wasn't so sure. There was a vulnerability about her, a sweetness even. That, coupled with her strength and determination, made a potent combination. One he admired. And one he had to admit would make for very few dull moments.

Not that his newfound appreciation of Tori the woman really mattered. He might be getting a glimpse of her, but he knew better than to think that Tori the agent let the woman get out and about very often.

Besides, to her, he was just the boss. Just her competition within the FBI. Although they might be sharing an amazing few hours, he had no reason to think that anything real had changed between them.

And, frankly, that was a damn shame.

FOR THE FIRST TIME in her sexual life, Tori wanted to kick back and chat after making love with a man. Unfortunately, it was almost five o'clock in the morning, and she'd outlasted this particular man by about an hour.

They'd made love over and over and over, until the condom box was nearly empty and Carter had begged for mercy and a nap. He was sleeping beside her, and she was basking in the memory of his touches.

By about their fourth round, she'd forgotten that their sexual marathon had started as a challenge. She'd wanted only to enjoy his touch, to lose herself in the moment...and she'd wanted to make sure he was enjoying himself as much as she was. No, that wasn't true. Tori wanted Carter to be even more lost than she was; she wanted him to experience the absolute heights of passion. To be lifted up to the sky and gently settled again.

And she wanted to be the one to take him there.

She'd never felt that way about a man before, and for the life of her, she couldn't decide if she was being incredibly giving or incredibly selfish. In the end, though, it probably didn't matter. All that mattered was her and Carter and the two or so hours left until dawn. Two perfect hours where she could simply snuggle with the man next to her and not worry about whether he was her superior or whether she was going to get the job or win the reputation she wanted. About whether she was ever going to fill her father's shoes.

Determined, she shoved the thought of her father out of her mind. She'd spent ninety percent of her life trying to fill his shoes. So far, she'd done a pisspoor job. Her father had been a man of action. A man who followed his own path and had always managed to end up exactly where he was supposed to be. Unlike her dad, the most action Tori had seen had been her fingers flying over a computer keyboard. At least until she'd hooked up with Carter. Ironic, considering that her rendezvous with Carter at Quantico was the very reason she'd seen so little action.

She snuggled closer, unable to help the broad grin that was spreading over her face. Tonight, anyway, she'd seen a lot of action. And chances were, as soon as they reached the resort, she'd see even more. Both in the bed and in the field.

She could hardly wait.

10

"I'M SORRY you'll be leaving us today." Phyllis reached past Carter to put a basket of biscuits on the table.

"So am I," Carter said. He meant it, too. After last night, he'd happily spend a few more nights with Tori in a small room dominated by a bed. Hell, there didn't even need to be a bed. He enjoyed verbally sparring with the woman as much as he enjoyed making love to her. He aimed a glance her direction. "We haven't even had the chance to check out your hot tub."

Tori had been pouring herself a cup of coffee at the sidebar, and she turned, shooting him a look filled with decadent possibilities. "Maybe we *should* stay an extra day."

He aimed an equally suggestive glance right back at her. "Sweetheart, I wish we could."

Phyllis patted his hand. "I'd love you to stay, of course, but the tub will still be here when you come back for your anniversary."

Tori set her coffee down, then concentrated on pulling out her chair. An attempt, Carter was sure, to hide her grin. "Our anniversary?" she said.

"Of course," Priscilla answered. "Either your first or your tenth. Or any one in between." She grabbed one of the empty chairs and sat down. "I do so enjoy it when newlyweds come here to stay. Honeymooners always brighten up the place." She flashed a smile

Tori's way, then aimed it right at him. "Especially a young couple that's as much in love as you two."

Carter opened his mouth—why, he wasn't sure. Certainly he couldn't argue. Not and risk blowing his cover. And, truth be told, he didn't really want to argue. He might not be in love with Tori, but he'd definitely passed lust on the emotional continuum.

"You two are just a delight to have around," Phyllis added. "There's a longing in your eyes I haven't seen since I saw it in my dear Edmund's eyes." She leaned back with a sigh, the expression on her face reflecting pure delight.

A wash of sadness swept over Carter, and he focused on the scrambled eggs and bacon on his plate. He told himself he was only feeling melancholy because Phyllis had lost someone she loved. But he was fooling himself.

No, the source of his melancholy was sitting across the table from him, staring deep into a cup of coffee and looking like she wasn't at all happy to be awake, even though it was already past noon. Most important from Carter's perspective, she didn't appear the least bit aware that somehow she'd completely gotten under his skin.

He thought about Phyllis's words. *Love.* More specifically, love and Tori. Shaking his head, he stifled a mirthless laugh. Tori wasn't the type who fell in love. And, he told himself, she certainly wasn't the type he'd fall in love with.

Except that was a lie. She was exactly his type, even though he hadn't wanted to admit it. Spirited and smart, a woman who knew what she wanted and wasn't afraid to go after it. The trouble, of course, was that what she wanted and what he wanted didn't mesh at all.

He wanted a woman who'd stick around. A woman who wanted a home and family. Not to mention a woman who didn't consider him the enemy. Maybe he'd been wrong about the night she'd run out on him, but he wasn't wrong about her competitive streak. It was bright neon and a mile wide.

And as delicious as last night had been, it was probably a mistake. Considering his and Tori's history, he could forgive himself the serious lapse of professionalism. His bigger mistake, however, had been giving in to Tori's competitiveness. She had some intense need to go one-on-one with everyone she met, and rather than try to back her off that tendency, he'd fueled the fire last night.

She'd beaten him, too. Fair and square. He'd been completely exhausted when they'd fallen asleep a few hours before dawn. Tori, of course, had still been raring to go.

Instead of being satisfied with her victory, though, Carter had the sinking feeling Tori would want more independence, not less. He'd hoped their closeness in bed would bring them some closeness on their team, but he feared that Tori's inability to be a team player was going to jeopardize their mission.

He hoped she'd prove him wrong. Hell, he wanted them to be a team. If anything, last night had proved to him they could work together. He and Tori had fit together like the pieces of a jigsaw puzzle. They'd anticipated each other's thoughts and predicted each other's desires. He'd never before felt that level of closeness with anyone, much less a woman, and he hoped like hell they'd have that kind of rapport in the field.

Even more, he hoped they could have it in real life.

"HEY, BUDDY!" Jonathan Barker slapped Carter on the back as he and Tori stepped into one of the private offices at the Santa Barbara County Sheriff's Department. "Long time no see."

Carter shook his friend's hand with enthusiasm. "How the hell are you? I didn't know you were in California."

"Been here two years now. When I heard you were working the task force, I called in a few favors and got assigned to the team."

Carter turned to Tori. "Jon and I worked together at the Waxahachie police department."

"About a million years ago," Jon said. He and Carter had been partners until Carter had made the decision to join the FBI. Jon had considered applying, as well, but as a single dad, it hadn't been feasible. The decision had made sense to Carter, of course, but he'd sorely missed his friend.

Jon turned to Tori and offered his hand. "Good to meet you. You're a brave woman going undercover with this rogue at a sex resort." Jon winked. "He's into method acting, you know."

"Really?" Tori said. "I guess I'll have to dig out my chastity belt. Wouldn't want to be ravaged in the night." Her voice might be typical Tori, but the slight blush gave her away. To most people, her reaction would probably go unnoticed. But Jon wasn't most people; he'd been famous in the department for reading suspects, for noticing the subtle indications that told him whether or not they were telling the truth.

Carter had no doubt Jon knew exactly what as going on between Carter and Tori. And when Jon turned ever so slightly Carter's way, Carter knew he'd nailed it.

"I don't know," Jon said, not missing a beat. "From what I remember, women far and wide were standing in line to be ravaged by the likes of Carter Sinclair."

"Really?" Tori raised an eyebrow, and Carter recognized that she was pulling herself together. Jon's initial comment had thrown her, but she was fighting back with a vengeance. "I guess there's just no accounting for taste."

Jon laughed. "Yeah, I know. Sorry you're stuck with him." He struck a pose and prodded his biceps. "Too bad I can't go in with you and have Carter stay here and keep the home fires burning."

Tori batted her eyelashes. "Oh, could you? I need a big strong man around to protect me."

At that, Carter couldn't hold it in any longer, and he burst out laughing. "Don't believe her, Jon. Tori's one woman who can take care of herself."

She turned to him, a surprised expression on her face. "You think?"

He frowned, taken aback at the question. "Hell, yes."

"Oh." She squinted, but didn't say anything further. Carter thought about asking what was on her mind, but Jon piped up.

"Tori *Lowell*," Jon said. "Now I recognize that name. You wrote the initial report."

"That's right."

"It's a pleasure to finally meet you. I've been impressed with your work."

She squinted at him. "You have? One report and you're impressed?"

"About six reports, actually." He leaned against the desk, one leg hooked over the corner. "I've worked with the FBI quite a bit on a number of white collar cases." He aimed an assessing nod in her direction. "You do a damn good job."

"Thank you," Tori said. Her words were gracious enough, but Carter thought he caught a hint of confusion flitting across her face. She licked her lips. "I actually enjoy the research. There's something satisfying about running down a trail of evidence and then putting it all together in one package."

"Well, you're damn good at it," Jon said.

Her eyes flicked toward Carter. "Thank you," she repeated, then shrugged. "Of course, it's not nearly as satisfying as being out there getting down and dirty with the bad guys, but some of us have to take what we're handed."

Jon looked from Carter to Tori. "I guess it all depends on what it is that floats your boat." He held up Tori's report and rifled the pages. "I mean, I sure as hell couldn't do this, but I'm damn envious of the work you do."

A flash of confusion crossed her face, and she avoided Carter's eyes, not looking at Jon, either. "Um, right. Well, about the report." She rummaged in her briefcase and pulled out a battered file folder. "Maybe I should make some copies for everyone before we get started. I made some revisions before we got here, so your version has changed. Nothing earth-shattering," she added. "Just some charts I created to show the various employees the victims came in contact with. I, uh, I didn't find any connections. Maybe someone else will."

Carter crossed his arms and leaned against the wall.

This was getting interesting. Tori wasn't known for suggesting that she might have missed something or that she might need help. And two days ago she certainly hadn't offered to pass him a copy of her charts for his perusal.

"There's a copy machine next to the coffeemaker," Jon said. Tori nodded and headed out of the office. As soon as she rounded the corner, Jon kicked the door shut and turned to Carter. "Well?"

"Well, what?" Carter asked, stalling.

"Since when did you start sleeping with your partners?"

"Suppose I deny it?"

"I'd know you were lying."

Carter laughed. "I always knew you were intuitive."

"Just one of my many skills." Jon buffed his fingernails on his shirt. "Unlike some people I know, though, I'm not too skilled with the opposite sex."

"I thought you had a thing going with that reporter for the Hill County paper."

"Going, going, gone." Jon shrugged. "For the best, I suppose. Not long after we broke up, I got the offer to come work out here."

"How's Tabitha liking California?" Jon's little girl had been four when Carter last saw her.

"She loves it. She's in third grade now and she wants a pony. They grow up so fast." He aimed a slanted look in Carter's direction. "Putting down any roots of your own?"

"I'm starting to think along those lines."

"Really?" Genuine surprise played over Jon's face. "It's hard to have a family when you're working undercover all the time."

"I figured that one out all on my own. If everything goes well, this is my last undercover job."

"Oh?" Jon shot a glance in the general direction of the copy machine. "And the lovely Agent Lowell?"

"There's nothing there, Jon. Attraction, yes. But that's it."

"Didn't look like nothing to me."

"Trust me," Carter said. "We've got a history. We both gave in to something that's been tempting us for a long time, but there's nothing permanent there."

"You sure about that?"

Carter nodded. Unfortunately, he was. During the time he'd spent with Tori, he'd managed to scratch away at the hard surface of her personality to the soft woman underneath. He liked what he'd found, and he wouldn't object to exploring a relationship with her. But what he wanted didn't mesh with reality. "I'm sure. This case presented a perfect excuse, and we just gave in to temptation." And that was a damn shame, too.

"Sometimes, that will lead you places you never thought you'd go." Jon smiled, wistful. "That's how it was with me and Sarah."

The way Jon had told it, he and Sarah had met at the library one Saturday afternoon and had been married in Vegas three weeks later. "I dropped a copy of *Great Expectations*," Jon had once said, "and when I stood up, there she was, the love of my life. I couldn't help it. She bent down to help me, and I shocked myself by kissing her." They'd had seven blissful years before cancer had taken her, leaving Jon with their little girl.

"Doesn't work that way for most people," Carter said.

Jon half shrugged. "Maybe. But it just might work

that way for you." He aimed a finger at Carter. "I saw the way you two look at each other."

"You saw lust," Carter said. "I'm not denying that. But she's not interested in more."

"And you?"

Carter grimaced. Wasn't that just like Jon to pick up on Carter's little omission? "I'm not, either," he said. It was a technically true statement even if, were circumstances different, he might be willing to pursue something. Maybe there was more between him and Tori than just a competitive history, but faced with their real lives, none of that mattered. "And even if we were, there are too many obstacles."

"Since when were you afraid of a few obstacles?"

Carter let that one pass.

Jon rolled his eyes. "Okay. I'll bite. What kind of obstacles?"

"Our jobs, for one. I'm looking to escape undercover work, and she's angling for an undercover assignment."

Jon's brow furrowed. "Really? She's wants a change?"

"You look surprised."

"That's because I am. I've been the liaison between the department and the Bureau several times now, and I've run across Tori's reports at least half a dozen times."

"So?"

"The woman's damn good at what she does. I'm surprised she wants to give it up."

"Trust me. She does."

Jon shrugged one shoulder. "Undercover agents do manage to have families. You two could still..." He trailed off, his voice rising with unspoken implications.

Carter's gut twisted. With any other woman, maybe. But not Tori. They wanted different lives, and the life she wanted didn't mesh with his. It just didn't. Hell, he'd known since kindergarten that you couldn't put a square peg in a round hole, no matter how hard you tried. And no matter how much you wanted to. So help him, he did want to. The one woman in all the world he shouldn't have—*couldn't* have—turned out to be the one he wanted.

But somehow, he didn't have the energy to explain that to Jon. Instead, he crossed his arms and shook his head.

"Mark my words, buddy," Jon said. "After spending some time at the Kama Resort... Well, who knows? Anything is possible."

"Anything except me and Tori," Carter said, the knowledge depressing him more than he wanted to admit.

"How do you know if you don't try?" Jon asked.

"Jon..." Carter laced his voice with a note of warning.

"I'm serious. You're clearly interested—"

"I'm not," Carter lied.

"Don't bullshit me, man. I know you too well. And I never thought I'd see the day when Carter Sinclair turned away from a challenge."

Jon turned to some paperwork, leaving Carter to consider that bomb.

Tori would resist, of course, but Jon was right—Carter really did love a challenge. And Tori definitely qualified as that.

He stood up straighter, letting the decision settle in his bones. Mentally, he nodded. It was a risk, true. But it was a risk he had to take. He wanted her, and damn it, he was going to fight for her.

Which left just one question—how the hell was he going to win?

THE SUN WAS LOW in the sky by the time they reached the Kama Resort, and Tori put away her notes as they drove past the gate. She turned to Carter, every cell in her body tingling with excitement over the prospect of her first real undercover mission. "Well, here we are."

"Nervous?"

She was, but she wasn't about to admit it. "Of course not. This is my job."

He laughed. "So? You can still be nervous."

She lifted her chin. "Well, I'm not."

"Uh-huh." He clearly didn't believe her, but instead of making her angry, his quiet disbelief warmed her. Carter understood how she was feeling. She'd never had anyone who could empathize with her, and the knowledge that he could was kind of nice.

"I remember how nervous I was on my first undercover assignment," he said. "Forget catching the bad guys, I just didn't want to throw up."

She laughed. "You're joking."

"A little," he said, sharing a smile with her. "But I really was nervous." He reached over and stroked her fingers. "But I got over it, and you will, too."

"You've had years to get over it," she said, immediately regretting sounding so snippy. She shrugged. "I mean, this is the first time they've let me out of my cage. Ironic that it's you I'm working with."

He frowned, the car slowing as he focused on her and not on driving. "That's the second time," he said.

"The second time what?"

"That you've said something that doesn't make sense," he said. "Earlier you said something about a tryst. About how our night at Quantico affected your career but not mine."

She nodded. "Exactly. It's a double standard, and it's not fair." She worked to keep the edge out of her voice. After all, even if Carter had gotten the benefit of that double standard, it wasn't his fault; he hadn't personally held her back.

"What isn't?"

"Someone *saw* us, Carter."

He shrugged, not looking particularly disturbed. "So? The Bureau frowns on dating, but it's not forbidden."

She half snorted. "No, they don't forbid it. They just screw up your whole career if they catch you."

He opened his mouth, but she cut him off, not wanting to hear whatever excuse he might have concocted on behalf of the powers that be.

"And your career is fine because you're a guy," she said. "Don't be naive."

"There's no double standard, Tori."

A spark of anger flared. "Of course there is. Why do you think you've always gotten the prime assignments while I've been stuck doing research?"

He shrugged. "Because you're good at it?"

"But it's not what I want," she said, trying to make him understand. "Every single one of my requests for assignment has been ignored. I'm not stupid, Carter. Someone saw us and, oh, my God, because I'm a woman, I'm getting screwed while you're getting promoted." She leaned back, her arms crossed over her chest, and fumed.

He shook his head. "You're wrong."

"Yeah? Well, that's your theory."

"Trust me, babe. I've seen your file." He turned just long enough to look her in the eye, and she saw the truth reflected there. "There's nothing in there about you and me. No plot. No conspiracy. No notations about how the Bureau is out to get Tori Lowell." He shrugged again. "Sorry."

Frowning, she turned to look out the car window. If Carter was right, then why had she been held back? Their story had always been that she didn't follow the rules, that she was a wild card. But that couldn't be the real reason. Her father had always played by his own rules, and his career had flourished.

The familiar fear settled around her. Was it that she wasn't good enough? Despite all her successes, was she failing where it really mattered? She steeled herself. *No.* There had to be another reason.

Murphy, maybe? Had her mentor and family friend intentionally held her back? There was no other explanation. If Carter was right, then Murphy had to be the reason. Well, fine. If that was the case, she'd work extra hard. She'd focus completely on this mission—she'd give it absolutely everything—and in the end, they'd have to give her another undercover assignment.

Twisting in her seat, she glanced at Carter. She'd given in last night. They'd both pretended that sleeping together was some sort of prep for their mission, but she knew the truth. She'd weakened. She'd used their competition as an excuse, and she'd loved every minute of it. She remembered the way his hands had felt on her body, the way he'd taken her to the absolute heights of passion and then brought her down again, just as soft as a feather.

It had been wonderful, but it needed to be over. She

needed to focus on the job, not on her libido. From here on out, she was only doing what was necessary for the mission. She had to succeed. She had to. And if that meant ignoring the way Carter touched her, the way his skin felt against hers. Well, then so be it.

She licked her lips, knowing she wouldn't be able to entirely ignore him. They were undercover at a sex resort, after all, and there had to be some sort of show for the public. But in private, well, they needed to concentrate on finding the bad guys. Not her G-spot.

And that was for the best. Because there wasn't anything real between them anyway. There couldn't be.

She didn't have any more time to think about it, though, because they were coming up on the resort's buildings. She pointed to a wooden sign next to the caliche drive. "That way," she said.

As he aimed the car that direction, she fought to get her mind off her past assignments and concentrate on this one. Jon had briefed them on what the task force knew. Other than what was in Tori's report, it wasn't much. They had a list of all employees, and they knew that someone had been hocking goods at the local pawn shop. A seemingly useless fact, but Jon had mentioned it to show how little they knew.

After the rundown, they'd gone over the plan—Tori and Carter would check in and spend the next couple of days trying to talk to as many potential suspects as possible while the off-scene officers would continue doing background checks on the resort's employees.

Unfortunately, none of Tori's charts had yielded any prime suspects. She hadn't figured they would; she'd combed the information herself several times, and nothing had turned up. She'd shared her research reluctantly, but she'd known it was necessary. And, frankly, she'd wanted to please Carter. So while she'd been proud of herself for sharing her work, she'd also been secretly happy that no one was able to discern a connection she'd missed.

Now that they were here, the plan was for them to report anything untoward. The team would investigate and, if necessary, send in the cavalry. Tori and Carter weren't supposed to do anything except be the project's little moles. Hell, they didn't even have their guns, a precaution in case the blackmailer was one of the maids who searched the rooms for incriminating facts.

Of course, Carter and Tori were also the bait. Throughout their stay, they were going to dribble out tidbits of personal information designed to entice an extortionist. Tori had to laugh at how decadent her imaginary sex life had become. First, they'd supposedly come to the resort to learn how to make their already amazing sex life better. Now, it turned out their amazing sex life included participating in an underground sex group, where husband and wife traded partners and a wild time was had by all.

Not the kind of life she'd want to lead in the real world—and if she was *really* married to Carter, she certainly wouldn't want to share him—but she supposed the concocted story made good blackmail fodder. Especially since their background story included Carter's very wealthy father who was not only the source of their considerable wealth, but was also planning to run for office in a conservative Texas city and couldn't afford a scandal.

When Jon had briefed them both on the details of their cover stories, she'd been impressed by how well the ruse had been set up. The Bureau had arranged a name, telephone number and company background for Carter's supposed father. It would take some serious digging for the perp to discover the truth.

As Carter headed for the main building, she watched the scenery. No doubt about it, the resort was beautiful. Several acres on the hills near Santa Barbara, the land must be worth a fortune. Of course, the owner, Tobin Seger, had a fortune. Not only had he started with family money, but his tapes and classes for couples looking to improve their sex life were incredibly popular and had netted him millions.

That alone was enough reason for Tori to shy away from Seger as a suspect. Since he clearly didn't need the money, why would he risk his future by blackmailing his clients?

They passed a series of cabins set back from the road, a tennis court and an Olympic-size pool before Carter finally pulled up and parked in front of the main building. Looking much like a giant, pink wedding cake, the building seemed to be a caricature of the stucco architecture so popular in southern California.

Carter parked the car, then turned to Tori with a shrug. "It's a sex resort, after all. Did we really expect subtle?"

He had a point. They headed up the granite stairs together, and somewhere along the way, Carter took her hand. They entered the building hand in hand and wandered through the empty hallway looking for the check-in desk. Along the way, they passed an office with the door partially open and a male voice coming from within.

"Maybe we should ask him," Tori said.

Carter started to push open the door, then stopped.

Tori peered over his shoulder and saw a frazzled-looking man with a salt-and-pepper beard talking on the phone.

"Next week, I promise," the man said, running his fingers through his hair, making it stand on end.

"We'll come back if we don't find the main office," Carter said, whispering as he stepped back from the door.

Tori nodded.

"Could you repeat that?" the man in the office said. "Really?...I thought it was more, but I guess you would know."

They walked away, wandering until they finally found the main office, then realizing they'd parked at the side of the building rather than the front.

As they walked in, a rotund man with a horseshoe of hair was rummaging through a file cabinet. Behind him, a twentysomething woman with wiry red hair transcribed dictation at one of the computers, a nameplate identifying her as Brandi resting on top of her monitor.

"Hello?" Carter said.

The man jumped a mile, but Brandi kept on typing, apparently absorbed in her work.

"Sorry."

The man put a hand to his chest. "Not to worry. You just startled me." He pulled a pair of glasses out of his front pocket and peered at them each in turn. "You must be the Davenports."

Carter nodded. "That's right. Carter and Tori Davenport."

The man stuck out his hand. "I'm Tobin Seger."

Carter fought his immediate reaction to raise an eye-

brow in surprise. Tori, apparently having the same reaction, squeezed his hand.

"Good to meet you," Carter said, shaking Seger's
hand.

"You look surprised," the man said.

"No, no." Carter and Tori traded a look, and Carter
knew exactly what she was thinking—that the man
must have been twenty years younger and with a tou-
pee when his publicity picture was taken. Carter had
studied that picture for days, and never once had he
expected a short, stocky, balding man. "It's just that we
didn't expect you to be working in the front office. I
guess I expected we'd be checking in with one of your
staff members."

Seger came to the counter. "Well, it's after five and
I'm here, so why don't we go ahead and take care of
that." He headed to the file cabinet and rummaged
some more, finally returning with a folder labeled
Davenport.

"Here we go," he said. "Ah, yes. You're in the A
group."

"The A group?" Carter asked.

"Achievers," Seger said. "You're here looking to
make something good better." He pulled a sheet out of
the folder. "Here's your itinerary. It lists all your
classes, workshops, encounter sessions. And, of course,
you're under no obligation. But you'll find that you get
the best results if you follow our suggested plan. And
on the reverse side, you'll find a list of the various other
classes and gatherings that take place from six to midnight."

Tori took the paper and started skimming it. Tantric
Sex. Erogeneous Zones. Fun with Toys. Everything

You Wanted To Know About Bondage, But Were Afraid To Ask.

Her cheeks heated, and she kept her eyes on the paper, afraid to look up in case Seger could tell from her eyes she was a fraud.

"Yes, about our itinerary," Carter said. He cleared his throat. "I'm not sure we're really, uh, achievers."

Tori turned to him. What the hell was he doing? They'd agreed on their role at the airport. Unless he'd seen the itinerary over her shoulder and was chickening out...

"Oh?" Seger asked.

"Yes. Well, you see. When we filled out the application...I mean..." He trailed off, then started again. "The sex is fine. But it's not fine. There's something missing." He aimed a fleeting glance at Tori. "We'd like to work on intimacy, not just sex."

"What are you—"

Before Tori could finish, Seger reached over the counter and took both their hands. "It's so refreshing to hear you say that. So many couples who come here just don't understand."

Tori frowned. "Understand what?"

"That without intimacy...without love...sex is just an aerobic activity. And not nearly as efficient as jogging, for that matter."

"But—"

"My studies have shown that a couple's sex life improves one hundred percent if they'll forget about working on the acrobatics of sex and instead concentrate on the psychology of sex. Communication. Intimacy. Those are the core ingredients of a good sexual relationship." He shrugged. "Of course, communication isn't easy. And no one wants to work. So they come here, looking for toys and the Venus Butterfly and who knows what. We can improve the sex, of course. But only you can improve the experience."

"I...oh." Tori had no idea what to say, so instead she turned to Carter, her mouth agape, wondering what the hell he was doing.

Seger snatched the sheet from her hands, then took a pen and began scribbling. "I'm booking you for tomorrow morning with Dr. Jim Garvey. Fabulous man. Wrote *The Marriage Team.* You may have heard of it. All about how marriage is a true partnership. And that team effort translates into the bedroom. Brilliant thesis. Wonderful man. You'll love him."

"Sounds great," Carter said.

Tori had no idea if he meant it, or if he was simply deep in his undercover role.

For her part, she was too perplexed to do any method acting. Whether that made her a lousy undercover agent or not, she didn't know. All she knew was that she wanted out of that building.

"Honey," she said, taking Carter's hand. "Maybe we should go unpack."

"Of course," Seger said. "You just got here, and I'm keeping you. Let me just get your key."

A few minutes later, he'd given them their key and a map of the grounds and was walking them to the door they'd entered through.

"I'm so pleased you and Tori are taking this step," Seger said with a slap to Carter's back. "Jim will work with you more tomorrow. Tonight, though, I'd like you to tell each other what you want."

Tori raised an eyebrow. "Excuse me?"

Seger just laughed, ignoring her question. "Go ahead, Carter. Tell Tori."

With a little nod, Carter turned to her, then took her hand in his. He looked at her, his eyes warm and gentle. "Tori, I want this marriage to work. We're a team, and I want us to be a real team. I don't want just sex. I want to make love."

His words shot straight to her core, and she gasped, more disturbed by her reaction than by Carter's speech. Carter, of course, had only been playing his role. In her mind, Tori knew that.

In her heart, though...well, her heart wanted to believe that Carter really meant the words he spoke.

That was a reaction she hadn't expected at all. And, frankly, it was a reaction that scared her to death.

11

"WHAT THE HELL did you do in there?" Tori whispered the second Seger reentered the building.

"Just my job," Carter said. He knew Tori would press the issue, but he'd foolishly hoped she'd wait until they were in their cabin.

"Your job is to discuss our sex life?"

"Under the circumstances, yes."

Tori glared at him.

"Garvey's famous for his intimacy training," he said. "And I took a shot that Seger would put us in with him if I laid that story on him."

"But why?"

"Talking," he said. "Tantric sex sounds pretty damn nice—"

Tori raised an eyebrow.

"—but how much talking do you think goes on in one of those kinds of classes? Someone is *talking* to our victims, Agent Lowell."

"And we might as well start with the sessions that have us talking, not touching." She nodded. "I get it."

"Yeah, well, don't get me wrong. I'm all for touching." He hooked his arm around her shoulder as they walked down the steps toward the car. She leaned against him, and the automatic nature of her response thrilled him even as he wondered if she was aware. He drew in a breath, gathering his courage. "There's more, too," he said, wondering if he was doing the right thing. His talk with Jon had jump-started his courage, but courage and wisdom didn't necessarily walk the same path.

"More?"

He steeled himself. "There's something between us, Tori. Something more than this assignment. And I want to explore it."

She stopped cold in the middle of the parking lot, then shrugged out from under his arm. "You what?" Her eyes opened wide, her voice straining with disbelief. All in all, pretty much the reaction he'd expected, although he'd hoped for something a bit less amazed and confused.

"You heard me," he said.

She started walking to the car again. "I guess I just can't believe my ears." After a few more seconds of walking, she turned on her heel and faced him. "There's nothing real between us, Carter. Last night was..." She trailed off, licking her lips. "Um, it was very nice. But I think we both know we were just competing. As always."

"Competition," he said. "Right. I should probably thank you for that."

One eyebrow quirked up. "Excuse me?"

"Competing with you. You're damn good, Tori. You can really drive a man to work harder."

Her mouth thinned, turning slightly down at the corners. She didn't say anything for a while, but her face softened, and he wondered if maybe he hadn't made an impact. Then she looked him in the eyes, and he knew he was dealing with the same stubborn Tori.

"Exactly," she said. "Just competition. There's nothing else between us."

He laughed. Typical Tori. He crossed the distance between her and took her hands. "I think you're wrong."

"Don't flatter yourself, Agent."

"Ah, but you forget," he said.

She pulled back from him, put one hand on her hip and gave him one of her looks. "What?"

"I'm a law enforcement officer. I'm trained to see things. I'm not flattering myself." He met her eyes, certain she saw the challenge in his. "There's something between us. I wasn't afraid to admit it. Are you?"

A muscle twitched in her cheek, and Carter forced himself not to smile.

"Admit it," he said. "There's a spark between us. Something real. Something I want to explore."

"It's just sex, Sinclair." She spoke firmly, looking him squarely in the eye. For a second, he almost believed her, and in that one second the world crashed down around his shoulders. Right then, he knew—he just *knew*—that he'd fallen hard for Tori Lowell. Not just for the way she felt in his arms, not just for sex, not just for their sparring. He'd fallen for *her*. And he also knew he'd do anything to get her.

He opened his mouth to say something—anything—but he never got the words out.

She leaned her head back and released a groan of pure irritation. After a moment, she put her face in her palms and rubbed before finally looking up. "Even if there is something there, nothing's ever going to come of it."

"Why not?" he asked, even as his heart leaped.

She released a loud breath. "I may have kept you on your toes at Quantico, but my skill didn't do me a damn bit of good. But now I'm finally getting the chance to do what I want, and it just doesn't jive with...well, with there being an *us*."

"You want an undercover assignment."

"Of course," she said.

"Why?"

She cocked her head. "What do you mean, why?"

"Because of your father? Or is there more to it than that? Because if there's not, I think you're making a big mistake."

Her eyes flashed. "You know, Carter, I don't recall asking your opinion on the matter."

Carter didn't intend to let her off that easily. "He broke every rule in the book."

"He solved his cases."

"Different era, Tori. And even if he was this stellar superagent, why emulate him? Was he ever really around for you and your mom?"

Her face hardened. "This isn't about him. I just don't want a relationship right now. I need to focus on my career."

"Yes, I agree. You do. But your career should track your talents. You have a knack for this research and analysis thing. You're a problem solver. Hell, you already have a reputation inside and outside the department. Look at Jon."

She shook her head. "He was just being nice."

"No, he wasn't. You're throwing away a career in something you like, in something you're good at, to try for a job you don't really know anything about."

Her jaw remained firm. "You know, for a second there, I was actually flattered. But now you're just being overbearing."

"Overbearing?"

"Yes," she said, her voice arctic cold.

Carter stifled a cringe, realizing he'd pushed too far, and a pissed off Tori was not a good thing.

"I know what I want, Carter."

Carter nodded, sure that she did. But he wondered if what she wanted was really to be an undercover agent. Or just to prove she could be as good as her dad.

Considering how strong-willed Tori was, if it was the second, he wondered if she'd ever admit she'd made a mistake.

He doubted it. And that was a damn shame.

THE MAN was infuriating.

As Carter aimed the car toward their cabin, she kept her eyes focused on the road. How dare he psycho-analyze her? She had her life completely planned out…and she was finally getting the opportunity to implement her plan.

She neither needed nor wanted his second-guessing.

As they reached the cabin, she looked sideways at him and exhaled. She might not want his advice, but he *was* right about one thing—she did want him. And it really pissed her off that he'd called her on that.

But wanting wasn't enough. She might want to eat chocolate for breakfast, but that didn't mean she was going to do it.

No, whatever was between her and Carter was going to have to remain out there in the ether someplace. The life she wanted was about to begin, and she didn't intend to sacrifice her plans or her future.

"We're here," he said, stopping the car and popping the trunk.

"Looks like it," she said.

"Listen, Tori—"

"We'd better get unpacked," she said, opening her door. "It's going to be dark soon."

He sighed but didn't argue, and for that Tori was grateful. She was still fuming, and she wanted some time to think without Carter in her head.

She slid out of the car and was heading for the trunk when she heard an odd noise. She looked at Carter, but he, too, appeared perplexed.

"Yoo-hoo! Over here!" A woman's voice, but Tori couldn't find the source.

"There," Carter said, pointing to a stone path a few yards behind them.

A man and a woman who looked to be eighty if they were a day strolled toward them.

"We're the official Kama Resort greeters," the woman said as they got closer. "And you are?"

Tori cast an amused glance toward Carter. "Tori and Carter Davenport," she said.

"Well, it's a pleasure to meet you," the woman said, shaking her hand vigorously.

"Don't mind Sheila," the man said, sticking out his hand toward Carter. "We're not really official greeters. We just come here so often, we feel like we're part of the staff."

"You're here a lot?" Tori said. If these folks spent much time at the resort, it was probably worth cultivating a friendship. Not to mention that they seemed pretty darned entertaining.

"Oh, my, yes," Sheila said. "Ever since Dr. Seger founded the place. We came for the first time on our fiftieth anniversary, and we've been coming every few months ever since." She leaned closer, whispering conspiratorially. "Dr. Seger gives us a break now. Of course, we told him we didn't want charity, but he called it a frequent flyer discount. Plus, he says we're a good advertisement for the geriatric crowd." She looked at her husband. "Do you know that Herb doesn't even need Viagra?"

Tori put a hand over her mouth to hide her grin, while Carter's eyes widened.

"You must be very proud," Carter said, but Tori could hear the laughter in his voice.

"Just good, clean living, son," Herb said. "You follow my advice and listen to Dr. Seger and the staff, and you'll be keeping your little lady satisfied on your eighty-second birthday, too."

Carter caught Tori's eye, the intensity there making her gasp. "I certainly hope so, sir," he said.

She shot him what she hoped was a warning look, but she had a feeling it wasn't too effective. Something in his eyes seemed so sincere it took a lot of the punch out of her righteous indignation.

He slipped his arm around her and pulled her close, his fingertip tracing down her arm. She tried to control her breathing but was having a hard time concentrating on anything except the sparks shooting through her body and the warmth pooling between her thighs.

"I'm surprised to see you," Tori said, trying to change the subject and get her mind on the case. "We haven't seen anybody on the grounds."

Herb put his arm around Sheila's waist. "Our cabin is the next one over," he said. "About a five-minute walk. And we knew someone was coming, so we kept a lookout. But other than that, you don't see many folks during the evening." He laughed. "For that matter, you don't see many folks during the day unless they want to be seen. That's one of the reasons this place is so popular with the rich and famous." He leaned forward, then lowered his voice. "Deniability," he said, in a heavy stage whisper.

Tori bit back a laugh. She knew she shouldn't make snap judgments, but she sincerely doubted Herb and Sheila were their blackmailers. And yet they'd focused on what made the resort such prime pickings for someone with that particular bent.

After a moment, Herb pulled Sheila close and kissed her ear. Watching their easy affection, Tori couldn't help but wonder if anyone would care enough to kiss her ear when she was eightysomething. Ironic, really, to be worried about the future when there was no one *now*. No one, that is, except Carter.

Pressing her lips together, she turned just enough to bring him fully into her field of vision. He was wrong about her father, but about everything else Carter was right on the money. No matter how much she wanted to deny it, she felt it, too. That pull between the two of them, like gravity only with electrical sparks. But she couldn't pursue it. Not and still feel like she had control of her life.

"Come on, kids," Sheila said, heading for their trunk. "We'll help you unpack. And then we'll take you to one of the evening classes. Herb and I are heading to sensual massage."

Tori stiffened as she imagined Carter's hands stroking and teasing her with warm oils and a firm touch. "Um, actually, we were going to just stay in and relax tonight. We don't—"

"We'd love to," Carter said. He grabbed their suitcases out of the trunk and led the slew of them into the cabin.

While Sheila and Herb waited in the little living room, Tori followed Carter into the bedroom. "Are you nuts?" she asked, even as she surveyed the room, checking for bugs. "We're not doing sensual massage. Not after—" She stopped, suddenly noticing the basket in the middle of the bed. "What is all this stuff?"

With some trepidation and more than a little curiosity, she crawled onto the bed and started pulling packages out of the red basket lined with pink and white tissue paper. "Lubricating jelly, a vibrator and some furry handcuffs." She held them up, letting them dangle. "Actually, these look kind of fun."

Carter chuckled. "Fine with me. We'll forget the massage and move straight to bondage."

Tori ran her tongue along the inside of her cheek. "Oh, no. Not after what you just said and what we did in Santa Barbara. I think it's best if we stay well away from massage and bondage and...and..." She held up the slim pink box. "And *vibrations*."

He took a step closer, his mere proximity intoxicating. "It's for the good of the mission, sweetheart. We meet people. We mingle. We act like we really belong here." He arched a brow. "That's the whole point of undercover work."

"But—"

"You *do* want to be an undercover agent. Right?"

Tori closed her mouth and exhaled loudly through her nose. "Fine. We'll do the massage. But the rest..."

Carter just smiled. He'd won this round. And he damn well knew it.

CARTER WASN'T SURE what the score was between him and Tori, but he knew he'd won their most recent round. And as they followed Sheila and Herb into the candlelit room, he was glad that he had.

The lessons were held in the instructor's cabin, and

they'd followed the elderly couple to the secluded building where they were greeted by Melinda, a stick-thin thirtysomething woman in a black bodysuit over which she wore a white men's suit shirt knotted at the waist. As Carter's eyes adjusted to the dim lighting, Melinda air-kissed all four of them, then invited them in with a hushed whisper.

As soon as they'd stepped into the large, open living room, Carter realized they weren't alone. About six other couples were there, spread out across the room on tumbling mats, an array of bottles and jars next to each station. The smell of peaches filled the air, and Carter noticed the bowls of potpourri scattered around.

"So glad you could join us," Melinda said, after Sheila and Herb introduced them. "Sheila, you and Herb take your usual mat, and Carter, why don't you and Tori take that mat by the fireplace?"

When they reached their mat, Carter realized how clever the setup was. While he'd been able to see most of the other couples from the doorway, now that he was on the floor he saw that Melinda had set up the mats around her various pieces of furniture in a way that provided maximum privacy. Of course, that left open the question of just *why* they needed privacy....

For some reason, he'd got it in his head that their newly acquired tour guides were taking them to a lecture. Apparently, though, this class was much more hands-on.

Not that he minded a little hands-on with Tori, but he'd rather hoped it would be in their cabin and, more particularly, in their bed.

As they knelt by the mat, though, another possibility occurred to him. Considering her recent refusal to even consider any sort of relationship with him, Tori might not be amenable to a repeat performance of their night at Phyllis's B and B. But if he could use this class as a way to jump start her interest...

He twisted the lid off a jar of scented cream and started rubbing it into his palms, more than ready to jump into the lesson.

Tori gave him one of her patented looks. "What do you think you're doing?" she whispered.

"Just getting ready," he said.

"No, no, no," she said. "If anybody's being the guinea pig, it's you." She scooted over to give him access to the mat. "You're as transparent as glass, and there is no way those hands are stroking my back or my *anything*." She crossed her arms over her chest, looking damn cute, too. "Just not happening."

He considered arguing, but from the look on her face, he wouldn't succeed. Besides, Melinda was clapping her hands and telling everyone to get settled. With Tori giving him the evil eye, he lay facedown on the mat, the rustling throughout the room suggesting that the other couples were doing exactly the same.

"Now, I realize some of you are new," Melinda said, "but tonight, I simply want you to go with the flow." Her voice, soft and melodious, drifted over then. "This is just to give you a basic idea of what sensual massage is all about. If you feel comfortable, take off your shirt. But if you'd rather wait until you're back in the privacy of your own cabin, that's fine, too."

Carter rolled onto his side and aimed a wicked grin at Tori. "Sure you don't want to take off that shirt?"

"Just lie down," she said, shoving at his shoulders.

"Yes, ma'am." He rested his head on his crossed

arms, his face turned just enough to watch her. Tori, of course, was ignoring him.

"When you get back to your rooms," Melinda said, "the first thing you'll want to do is set the mood. I've already started that for you with the candles, but you might also use incense, soft music, whatever you find romantic and sensual."

"Remind me to put on my Rolling Stones CD when we get back," Tori whispered.

Carter laughed. "Only if you play 'You Can't Always Get What You Want.'"

She turned, but not before he heard her sputter as she swallowed a laugh. Excellent. He'd just racked up one more point in his favor.

"Okay," Melinda continued, "your initial goal is to stimulate your partner's skin. What I want you to do is sweep the muscles of your partner's back and his or her legs and arms. Keep the touch light, folks. You're going for sensual here. Not working the kinks out of some football player's back."

Carter closed his eyes, waiting for Tori's touch. And waiting. And waiting. After a few seconds, he opened them and saw her sitting on her heels reading the ingredient label on one of the bottles. He cleared his throat.

"What?" she whispered.

"Sexually enthralled, remember?"

"We're *clothed*. This is pretend." She leaned closer. "And for us, it's pretending while we pretend."

"Yes, but—"

She cut him off with a little salute and a quirk of her lip. "Fine. You're right. You win again."

As Melinda's soft voice guided the group, Tori straddled his back and pressed her hands on his shirt near his shoulder blades. Her body was stiff, her motions jerky, and he could tell she was doing her best not to get lost in the exercise.

Melinda walked through the room, her voice filling the dark space. "When you're ready, concentrate on your partner's body. You want to entice and please. Pay attention to each muscle. Be firm, yet gentle."

As Melinda spoke, Tori rubbed her hands along Carter's back. He tensed, trying not to react to her too-light touch that tickled like he couldn't believe. He considered calling her on it—maybe even getting Melinda over to show what she was doing wrong—but he decided against it. He knew Tori well enough to know she was having to fight to keep her distance. If he was just patient...

"Excellent work," Melinda said. "You're all doing fine." She tiptoed by their mat, her stocking feet barely making a sound on the floor. "Remember, light but firm."

The pressure of Tori's touch increased, and Carter stifled a groan. The feel of Tori's hands on his back was intoxicating, and he silently thanked Melinda for kicking into gear Tori's need to be the star pupil.

"And don't forget about the lotions and oils. Those will give you better glide."

Carter turned his head. "Shall I take off my shirt so you can try the oils?"

"Thanks, but no thanks."

Stifling a grin, he turned his face to the mat, simply laying there and enjoying Tori's touch until Melinda turned off the music.

"Let's take a short break," she said. The second the words were out of her mouth, Tori was off Carter. "Refreshments are on the sideboard," she added, pointing to the far side of the room.

Tori met his eyes. "Mingle and talk?"

He wanted to say no—Tori was the only one he wanted to talk to—but they needed to work on the investigation, so he nodded. "Go for it."

She was gone before he'd even gotten the words out. They split up and, for the next fifteen minutes, both worked the room, chatting with the various men and women. Other than some fabulous cookies hidden behind a bowl of berries, however, Carter didn't discover anything even remotely interesting. Hopefully Tori had more luck.

When Melinda clapped her hands, they returned to the mat.

"Anything?" he asked.

She hesitated, then took a deep breath. "Nothing."

He laughed. "Don't worry. You're not a failure. I didn't learn anything useful, either." He squeezed her hand. "A lot of this job is tedious. Lesson number one."

"Everyone ready for another session?" Melinda asked.

Carter looked at Tori. "Of course, *this* part isn't tedious."

She rolled her eyes. "Just lie down."

He was starting to comply when Melinda spoke. "This time, let's change partners. Those of you who were massaging last time, get down on the mats."

Carter sat up.

"We don't have to do what she says," Tori said, her eyes reflecting concern. Smart girl. Carter definitely intended to get the most out of his new role of masseur.

"Yeah," he said, sliding off the mat and gesturing for her to lie down. "I think we do."

She opened her mouth, then shut it again, apparently deciding it was useless to argue. She rolled facedown on the mat. As Melinda turned on a tape of a babbling brook, Carter ran his fingers down Tori's back over the thin cotton of her shirt.

She sighed, and he decided to take that as an invitation. When his hands reached her waist, he broke contact just long enough to bathe his palms in one of the scented oils next to their mat. He didn't even bother to look at the bottle, so he was surprised when he caught the tropical scent of coconut.

Tori would object, of course, so he didn't bother to ask permission. He slipped his hands under her shirt, letting his skin glide over hers. At first she stiffened, and he heard her sharp exhale, but then her muscles relaxed under his touch and he knew he'd scored at least a minor victory.

With firm, even strokes, he massaged her back, caressing every inch of skin. Her breathing settled into a slow and easy pattern, and he would have thought she'd fallen asleep if it wasn't for the little moans of pleasure that escaped her every few minutes.

Emboldened, he unfastened the hook of her bra, drawing the pieces away to make room for his explorations. She gasped but didn't protest, and Carter silently thanked Melinda for providing such a wonderful excuse to touch her.

He let his fingers slide over her, grazing her sides and caressing the curve of her breasts. Her breathing increased in tempo, becoming faster as he slipped his hands into the cups of her bra, his fingers finding her nipples. He caressed and teased, delighting in the way her body squirmed beneath his, as if she were doing her best to hold in the urge to roll over and offer her body up to him.

He could have touched her all night, but the slow increase of light into the room interrupted. "This was great, people," Melinda said, as soon as the light returned fully. "We're out of time, but why don't you all go back to your cabins and enjoy what you've learned."

"You heard what Melinda said," Carter said, sliding his hands down her back, his fingers curved around her side just enough to stroke the swell of her breasts. "It's time to go back to our cabin." He kissed the base of her neck, delighted when she shivered under his touch. "Poor us...teacher's assigned a night full of homework."

12

SHEILA AND HERB conveniently disappeared during their walk back to the cabin, and Tori couldn't decide if she was upset or very, very grateful. Carter's revelation that he wanted to explore the attraction between them had thrown her off, and she'd hoped to have some time alone—time to get her head together.

No such luck. Even now, with only his hand on her waist as they walked down the path, her body tingled from his touch.

He'd teased her earlier and now, damn her, she wanted more. Which, of course, was exactly what Carter had been planning.

She should refuse. As soon as they got to their cabin she should go into the bedroom, toss him a pillow and a blanket and point him toward the couch.

That's what she ought to do. Hell, that's what she'd promised herself she would do.

Instead, she stopped cold and turned, one hand on her hip. "Only while we're here," she said, knowing her comment was out of the blue.

"Hello to you, too."

"I mean it," she said.

"I believe you," he said. His voice was perfectly serious, his face stern. Only the twitch in his cheek revealed his amusement. "But what are we talking about?"

"We can—" she twirled her hand in the air "—you know." She swallowed, unsettled by how much she wanted this man. She'd sworn to herself she'd have nothing more to do with him, but already she was compromising. But no man had ever touched her the way he'd touched her. And she had to be in his embrace once more. Even if only for a finite period. She wanted his touch almost as much as she wanted her new assignment. And that was what really scared her.

"But only while we're here," she said, determined to stick to her guns. "On the resort. And on the job. Once it's over, it's over. Deal?"

"Absolutely. So long as I can try to change your mind...absolutely."

She shook her head. "No, no, no. This is *it*. No pressure. Just us."

"No, thanks." He started walking again, moving past her down the path.

Her eyes widened, and she hurried after him. "Excuse me?" He kept walking. "Carter!" Still nothing. She jogged ahead and grabbed his shirttail. "Damn it, Carter. Stop."

He did, turning to face her. "What?"

"What are you doing?"

He shrugged. "You want a fast affair, I want something more. If you're not going to at least let me try to persuade you over to my way of thinking then I don't want to play."

Closing her eyes, she rubbed her temples. Had she thought he was infuriating before? She'd been wrong. *This* was infuriating.

"Has anyone ever told you you're insufferable?" she asked.

"Pretty much every day," he said.

She sighed. She ought to walk away. And she would have, too. But then he reached out and stroked her cheek. His fingers, warm despite the cool night air, burned against her skin. He traced lower, stroking her neck, his hand cupping the back of her neck. And then, before she knew it, he'd tilted her head and was kissing her.

And not just any kiss. This one was possessive. Intense. This was the kiss of a man who knew what he wanted and had the ego to believe he could get it.

Unsettled, she pulled away.

"What's the matter?" he asked. "Afraid?"

"Of your kiss? I don't think so."

"That I'll win? That I'll convince you to explore this thing between us even after we leave the resort?"

She was, actually. The tension between them kept growing, like a rope being pulled taut. Soon she was going to have to sever the rope or it would keep tugging her closer and closer to him.

At the same time, she couldn't admit that fear to him. And it wasn't as if she'd cave simply because he wanted her to. She had goals she intended to reach. She wasn't about to sacrifice all that just because she enjoyed sleeping with the man. She'd sever the rope eventually, but that didn't mean she had to do it now.

Licking her lips, she broke their embrace, looking first at the ground, then into his eyes. There was passion reflected there, a longing she wanted to lose herself in. Even if only for a few days.

Her breath trembled as she exhaled, and she lifted onto her tiptoes, hooking her arms around his neck and brushing her lips softly over his. "All right," she whispered. "Let's see if you can convince me."

THEIR CABIN was well-stocked with candles, and Carter made sure he found and lit every one of them. He didn't just want to sleep with Tori. He wanted to make love to her. To cherish her. To romance her.

He didn't know if he was in love with her—that was something he wasn't quite ready to face—but he did know that the possibility of love existed. And that was a possibility he wanted to explore with Tori beside him every step of the way.

She returned from the kitchen with a bottle of wine and two glasses. As soon as she'd set them on the table, she looked him in the eye. "You're certainly pulling out all the stops."

Her voice was amused, but the way her hands were playing with the hem of her shirt let Carter know that underneath her confident exterior, she was nervous. The knowledge moved him. If it was just sex, why be nervous? They'd done that, already. No, Tori was nervous because her heart was involved. She was falling, as he was.

And Carter intended to catch her.

Of course, the sword was double-edged. He was just as nervous. It was a night for seduction, and he had no idea how to start. He'd never once had that problem with a woman before, and that little fact spoke volumes. Tori was different. In so many ways, she was different from any other woman he'd dated.

And he wanted her more than any woman he'd ever been with.

Steeling himself, he moved toward her. When he reached her, he poured them each a glass of wine, then passed one to her. "To winning," he said.

Her smile told him he'd said the right thing, somehow broken the ice, and they clinked glasses. He knew he should sip, but instead he gulped the woody red wine, letting the fire of alcohol shoot through his veins, the heat nothing compared to the way his blood was boiling in anticipation of Tori's touch.

Reaching out, he stroked her cheek. "Teacher said we had homework, remember?"

She nodded. "I remember." She pressed her lips together, then looked at him. "And I always was a good student. I'd hate to disappoint one of my teachers."

"Then we better get to work. I have a feeling this assignment could take all night." He held out a hand, and she took it, her fingers firm and steady against his. "You're sure?"

She aimed a cocky smile his way. "About you finishing my massage? Oh, yeah. I'm sure."

He laughed, popping her lightly on the butt. "In that case, go lie down on the bed."

She saluted, then headed toward the bedroom. At the doorway, she looked back. "Bring the wine," she said.

He complied, then followed her into the bedroom. What he saw there just about stopped his heart—*Tori.* Stark naked, facedown on the bed.

Her skin glowed in the candlelight, and he stood there for a moment, doing nothing more than watch her breathe as the flickering light played along the smooth skin of her back and thighs.

He must have made a sound, because she twisted, looking at him, a challenge reflected in her smile. "I didn't want you to get oil on my clothes," she said.

"Makes sense to me," he said. He willed his feet to move, reminding himself that touching her would be so much more satisfying than watching her.

Her smile encouraged him, and he sat on the bed beside her. The heat from her body seemed to radiate to his fingers even before he touched her, and when he did put his hands on her back, a fiery passion seemed to envelop them both.

He groaned, undone by the overwhelming need to touch her, to enter her. Maybe it was the wine, but he suspected it was the woman, and he ran his hands languidly down her body, delighting in the shiver it produced.

"You're teasing," she said.

"Maybe a little."

"Well, don't."

He laughed. Even now she wanted to call the shots. "Yes, ma'am," he said. Leaning over her, he grabbed the toy basket off the bedside table, rummaging until he found the bottle of oil the resort had left for them. He started to unplug the top when she mumbled something.

"What?"

He felt her body lift as she took a deep breath. "I said, your dry cleaning bill will be horrendous."

He grinned. "Good point." It took him no time at all to escape the confines of his outfit.

With his clothes in a heap on the floor, he straddled her, every atom in his body straining with only one purpose—to touch her. To please her. He poured a dollop of oil into his palm, then rubbed his hands together, thrilled when the oil seemed to heat from the friction.

Leaning over, he stroked her shoulders, his movements smooth and measured. She wriggled beneath him, and he knew she wanted the touch as much as he did.

"Please," she whispered.

"Please, what?"

"Don't stop." Her voice, breathy and desperate, tantalized.

"I don't intend to." He slid his hands lower, until her entire back was slick with the oil. "Tell me what you like," he said.

"This," she said. "I like this."

While his hands stroked her back, he leaned forward to whisper in her ear. "See? That wasn't so hard."

"What's that?"

"Opening up to me." He traced his hand over her butt to stroke her hot, wet core. "Touch can do amazing things to people. It's powerful."

She moaned, then turned her head just enough to aim a mischievous smile at him. "It's powerful, all right, but you haven't won yet." She spread her legs. "But opening up? Maybe."

He laughed, her spunk delighting him as he stroked her arms. When her muscles sagged beneath him, he moved to her back, then her legs, trying to completely relax her.

Her breathing was slow and even, and he slid up, using his whole body instead of just his hands. He rubbed against her, his body tightening as she moved beneath him. So much for a relaxing massage; this one had them both on edge.

He wanted the moment to last, wanted it to build, but at the same time, he wanted her. He'd never before been so overcome with need, and the compulsion to give in to it was overwhelming.

Sliding down, he stroked the inside of her thighs, spreading her legs apart as he did. He slipped his body up, becoming even harder as he anticipated his purpose and his prize. And when his mouth reached her ear, he whispered, "I want you now."

She inhaled, her breath little more than a tremble of air, but she didn't protest. On the contrary, she spread her legs in silent invitation, and with one swift movement, he lost himself in her sweetness. She cried out, a sound of pure pleasure as she urged him not to stop.

Never. He'd never stop. And right then, he knew with absolute certainty that he'd entered into a competition with Tori he simply couldn't lose. He'd fallen for her. Fallen hard. And no matter what, his relationship with Tori was going to continue after this assignment.

No matter what, their relationship was going to be real.

THEY MOVED TOGETHER, so close that Tori couldn't tell where he ended and she began. She thrust against him, her knees and elbows pressed into the bed, as his hand reached down, stroking her intimately even as he thrust deeper and deeper inside her. She bucked against him, a steady heat building in her, growing hotter and more intense until she couldn't stand it any more and she cried out, her whole body singing as she collapsed onto the bed.

Carter lay on top of her, his weight and warmth comforting as a deep exhaustion spread through her body. Her release had been intense, almost painful, and she wanted nothing more than to roll over and embrace the man who'd brought her to the brink and back again. A man, she had to admit, who meant more to her than just a partner.

A small voice in her head told her she was falling in love, but she tried to ignore it. She didn't want to be in love. She had her career to think about, and love didn't fit the mix.

"Hey? You awake?" His soft whisper tickled her ear.

"Mmm." She snuggled closer. "I'm awake."

"Good." He traced a finger along her side, the lazy motion making her body tingle once again. "I'd hate to think you'd fallen asleep on me just when we were getting started."

A shiver of anticipation raced up her spine. *Just getting started.*

With slow, purposeful motions, he ran his hands over her back, the gentle pressure comforting. She started to roll over in his arms to face him, but he murmured, "No. Not yet." His hand continued its journey as his body pressed closer. He eased his hand over her side to cup her breast, then teased her with soft strokes before becoming bolder and more demanding.

He flattened his palm, running it over her tight nipple. As if she had a wire stretched from her breast to her core, a tingle of heat and desire ripped through her. She shifted, spreading her legs ever so slightly in a futile effort to find some release. But without Carter, there was no release to be had.

He knew what she needed, of course, and he traced his hand down, his fingers touching and stroking in a sensual rhythm that was exactly what she wanted. Almost.

"You," she murmured, almost unable to speak as the pressure built inside her. "I want you."

He complied without argument, just as she knew he would. In one strong motion, he turned her over, his lips teasing her ear, her throat, as she wriggled and moved beneath him seeking more. More touch. More *Carter.*

"Now?" he whispered, a tease in his voice.

She could only nod, lifting her hips to meet him as he thrust deep within her. She moaned as they rocked together, that wire inside her becoming tighter and tighter until, finally, it snapped in a frenzy of sparks and colors.

Gasping, she collapsed against him, her body limp, but somehow feeling fuller than she ever had. And she wanted more. Like an addiction, she had to have Carter again. Had to have her fill because once they left the resort, that would be the end of it. *Unless he won.* She pushed the thought away. He couldn't win.

Maybe she was falling for him, but that didn't matter. Love wasn't enough. She had her plan, and she didn't intend to deviate from it.

She took a deep breath. Time enough to think about that later. Right now, she wanted Carter. Right now, she didn't want their night to end.

Nibbling on her lower lip, she crawled over him and started rummaging through the basket. After a few seconds, she pulled out the fuzzy handcuffs and dangled them in front of him. "Ready for round three?" she asked, a challenge in her voice. "Or have I won again in the stamina department?"

Carter glanced at the clock on the table. "You might win in the end, sweetheart, but we're not there yet. I've got a few more hours left in me," he said.

"Good," Tori said, leaning forward to kiss him on the nose. "That's exactly what I wanted to hear."

13

"COME IN, COME IN." Dr. Garvey ushered Tori and Carter into his brightly lit cabin.

For a second, Tori paused in the doorway, trying to figure out why the doctor looked so familiar. And then it hit her—she'd seen him when they'd checked in. They'd overheard his phone conversation before they'd located Dr. Seger.

She took another look at him. Earlier, he'd seemed somewhat frazzled. Now he looked like he might have wandered down from Berkeley. He wore a pullover shirt and a gray wrinkled cardigan, his academic appearance topped by rectangular wire frame glasses.

"Please," he said, gesturing to a pile of throw pillows on the floor. "Have a seat."

Tori and Carter exchanged glances, then sat on the plush pillows, trying to get comfortable.

Garvey took the pillow opposite them, then offered them tea or coffee from the service on the low table between them.

"This isn't what I expected," Carter said. "Aren't we supposed to be laid out on couches discussing our dreams?"

Garvey laughed. "I'm not intending to analyze you. I just want you comfortable so we can start a dialogue. The key to better sex is better communication."

Tori felt her cheeks warm. Talking about her sex

life—especially when, until recently, it had been pretty much nonexistent—wasn't exactly an everyday occurrence for her. But it was part of the job, and she needed to keep that in mind.

Taking a deep breath, she faced Garvey. "Our sex life is fine." She shot a look toward Carter. One she hoped communicated that since the sex was fine, they really didn't need to explore any other aspects of their so-called relationship. "Personally, I don't have any complaints at all."

"No? Well, let's start there. Tell me about your sex life."

"I really don't—" She sat up straighter, totally defensive.

"See," Carter said, "this is exactly my problem. We're married, but we just can't seem to talk about these things." He took her hand, which annoyed her even more. "Tori, darling, I love you." One eyebrow arched ever so slightly. "We need to talk about our relationship. That's why we're here. Remember? You promised to try to talk when we saw Dr. Garvey."

Realization wonked her in the head. "Oh, sweetie, I'm so sorry." She leaned over and kissed him on the cheek. "You're right. I did promise to try."

She felt like kicking herself. She'd been so wrapped up in her feelings for Carter Sinclair, she'd completely forgotten that while they were at Dr. Garvey's, he was Carter Davenport. The point of this exercise wasn't to psychoanalyze her and Carter, but to try ferret out information about the blackmailer. And that meant leaking juicy information about Tori and Carter Davenport.

"No need to apologize," Garvey said. "Just tell me what it is you find satisfying."

She pressed her lips together. The fact was, acting wasn't one of her top ten talents. She worked better if she had a piece of paper, a computer and a database. Time to sort it all through. To think. To plan.

But she didn't have that right now, because both Carter and Garvey were staring at her. She had no idea what Tori Davenport would say, so she opted to answer for Tori Lowell. "The intensity," she said. "It's like being lost in a dream."

"Good," Garvey said, and she sat up a little straighter, feeling a bit like a first grader who'd just correctly added two and two. "What else?"

"Spontaneity," she said. "When we've made love, it's like...I don't know. Like a brushfire that starts from a single spark and then just takes over."

"But she holds back," Carter said.

"No, I don't," Tori said. "Not in bed."

"Ah, but can you really separate your sex life from the rest of your life?" Garvey asked.

She could, of course. But her alter ego couldn't. So Tori kept her mouth shut.

"It's not possible," Garvey continued. "You're a team. Two halves of a whole. And as such, your daily life and your sex life are always intertwined."

Carter didn't even bother to hide his smirk. "That's what I've been telling her."

Tori managed to rein in her desire to toss a not-so-polite retort right back at him.

"I think it's very interesting that you used a brushfire analogy," Garvey said.

"Why's that?" Carter said, beating Tori to the punch.

"Because of the underlying implications." He nodded toward Tori. "You say your sex life is fine, and yet you choose as an analogy something that destroys the landscape. Fire.''

"No, no," Tori said. "I just picked that out of a hat. I didn't mean anything by it."

"But that's my point. It's your subconscious talking to us. There's something you're afraid of destroying if you allow yourself to fully connect with your husband."

Garvey got up from his pillow and moved to the one beside her, then took her hands. Tori licked her lips and sank back. On the other side of her, Carter stayed completely stoic, but she was certain he was having the time of his life watching Garvey pick her apart.

"But Tori," Garvey said, leaning in even closer, "fire can also purify and cleanse. And even brushfires clear away the old brush to make way for new growth."

She sat there, a smile plastered on her face, wondering when they'd walked into touchy-feely land. Not only that, but they were getting touchy-feely about her life, not about Tori Davenport's. And she didn't like that at all.

After a few seconds, she glanced toward Carter, silently seeking help, but he looked to be holding in laughter and was totally useless to her.

"It's the sex clubs," she blurted.

Carter looked at her, his eyes wide. But she shrugged. She had to say *something* to get Garvey out of her face. And it worked, too. He let go of her hands and leaned back, a puzzled expression on his face.

"Excuse me?"

She stood up and started walking around his office, her fingers trailing over the knickknacks. A bowl of peach potpourri. A fertility goddess. A small fishbowl with a single goldfish. She frowned when she reached the bookshelves and noticed the record albums. She tried to get a handle on what was bugging her, but Garvey interrupted her thoughts.

"Tori? Sex clubs?"

"These clubs we go to back home," Carter said, getting into their role. "You know, different couples."

"Carter likes that kind of thing," Tori said, shooting him a sweet smile. Served him right for getting her into this mess. "And I like the sex, too, of course," she added, remembering their cover story. "But it's hard to get close to your husband when he's with another woman."

"That's very true, Carter," Garvey said, thankfully turning his attention from Tori to Carter.

Carter glared at her, but she upped the wattage on her smile.

"And it's even worse that we have to go to clubs in other cities," Tori added.

At that, Carter sent her a tiny nod of acknowledgment, and she patted herself on the back for opening the door to planting the bait. "Because of my father," Carter said. "The whole family, actually. If anyone found out, well, it would ruin us."

"The Davenports are very..." Tori trailed off, flicking her nose up. "And with Carter's dad running for office...well, you can imagine the hell that would break loose."

Garvey looked at his watch. "We're out of time, but my initial thought is for you two to take a vacation from visiting the clubs. Concentrate on each other instead." He moved to the far side of his desk and ran the tip of his pencil down the open page of his day planner. "So, how's tomorrow at three look for a follow-up?"

Carter and Tori exchanged glances, and then he put his arm around her shoulder. "We'll be here, Doctor. Tori and I are motivated. We're going to make this relationship work if it kills us."

"I MEANT IT, you know," Carter said, watching her.

Tori was on the bed, her notes spread out in front of her. She looked at him, her expression blank. "Meant what?"

He stifled a sigh of exasperation. "I want to make this work, Tori." He waved a hand between the two of them. "You and me. This. *Us.*"

Her eyes bored into his. "We've talked about this, Carter. We want different things."

"It can work, Tori. If we want it badly enough, we can make it work."

She frowned. "Please. Can't we be happy with the deal we made?"

He knew he should say no and walk away. They'd put on a public front and now, in the privacy of the cabin, he should turn away. If she didn't want something real between them, then what was the point?

He sighed. The point was, he had no self-control. He wanted her; hell, he craved her. And, somewhere in the back of his mind, he had the stupid idea that eventually she'd come around. Eventually, Tori would decide that he was the man for her and they'd live happily ever after. But, as Carter's grandfather would say, Tori was a stubborn cuss, and he should know better than to fantasize that Tori would ever willingly shift gears after she'd made up her mind one way.

He ran his fingers through his hair. He'd never considered himself a foolish man, but on this one point, reality seemed unable to penetrate his brain.

From her perch on the bed, she looked at him, a question in her eyes. "Carter?"

"So help me, Tori, you're driving me nuts." He moved to sit beside her, then reached out and stroked her cheek. "I always thought I was strong, but with you..." He trailed off, his fingers tracing the curve of her neck.

Her lips parted, and he knew he wasn't imagining the longing he saw reflected in her eyes.

"Call me an optimist," he said, "but I'm going to keep trying."

"It's not—" she began.

But he didn't let her finish, just closed his mouth over hers. Her lips met his, her mouth hot and ready, her tongue seeking entrance.

He shifted, moving to straddle her, and she helped him along, brushing her papers to the floor with a wild swing of her hand.

"Please," she whispered, her hands fumbling at the button of his jeans.

Her voice, filled with need, aroused him even more, and he strained against the denim. She was as desperate as he was, and the knowledge filled him.

"You want me," he said, looking into her eyes.

She nodded. "Yes," she said, then hooked her arms around his neck.

He took her answer and held onto it. His head knew that she'd only meant she wanted him for now, for sex. But his heart...

Well, his heart intended to believe that when she'd said yes, what she really meant was forever.

"You look relaxed, dear," Sheila said.

"Oh, yeah," Tori said. Of course, it was probably

hard not to look relaxed after two hours in a yoga class. She was relaxing next to the pool while Carter was taking a nap in their cabin. She smiled. Over the last few days, their late-night escapades had turned into late night *and* early morning *and* mid-afternoon escapades. And all that sex took a lot out of a guy. Tori, of course, had stamina.

Melinda walked by, deep in conversation with a redhead who looked vaguely familiar. She searched her memory for a second before remembering Brandi from the main building. Tori waved, but neither woman noticed.

"What are you up to?" she asked, turning to Sheila and looking at the woman over the rim of her sunglasses.

"Knitting," Sheila said. She held up a bag stuffed with colorful yarn.

"Really?" Tori bit her lip. So far the Kama Resort hadn't turned out to be what she'd expected at all. True, there were sex toys in the room where a hotel would leave chocolate, but no one was running around naked offering to find her G-spot. Everyone seemed normal and serious. And, Tori supposed, old ladies who knitted between sensual massage and Tantric sex classes were just par for the course.

"I'm quite good," Sheila said. "We sell my scarves at my grandson's store in Big Bear. Gives us a little extra pocket cash, and it certainly beats hocking my jewelry."

Tori sat up straighter. "What did you say?"

"Oh, I was only joking, dear. I would never pawn my rings."

She slapped her palm onto her thigh. *Of course!* Jumping up, she grabbed her bag and then clasped

Sheila's hands. "Thank you, Sheila. You've just made my day."

WHEN CARTER woke from his nap, his hand immediately snaked to the pillow next to him as he searched for Tori. Empty. Then he remembered. It was the afternoon. They'd made love. He'd been too zonked to move, and she'd bounced out of bed, ready to go jogging or some such nonsense.

Well, more power to her.

They'd been at the resort for four full days, and Carter was falling harder and harder for Tori with each passing day. That she had enough energy after sex to go exercise was only one more impressive item to add to his ever-growing list.

Stretching, he pulled himself out of bed. He almost wished he could stay there all day, but since Tori had left, he didn't really see the point.

Such a short period of time had passed, and yet since this mission had started his world had been turned upside down. He still wanted the same things—an assignment to a field office, a house, a dog.

A wife.

Only now he knew who he wanted that wife to be.

Since Tori had thankfully reined in her Rambo act and hadn't pulled any stunts, Carter figured he had a decent shot at getting the reassignment. The open question was whether he had a decent shot at getting the wife.

Still, he never bet against the home team, so his money was still on him.

Tori would come around. Already, she was opening up to him. While he would never knock their marathon sex sessions, they had to rest sometimes, and during those moments, he would hold Tori close and they'd talk. About life, the Bureau. Hell, once they'd even gotten into a knock-down, drag-out about which of the *Star Wars* films was the better movie. He'd voted for the original, but Tori's money had been on *The Empire Strikes Back.* Which, Carter thought, was lame considering *Empire* made you wait years to find out what happened to Han Solo.

He loved sparring with her. Hell, he loved her. And he knew she loved him right back. If it wasn't for her ambition and her father...

Stifling a yawn, he wandered into the bathroom and saw the mirror. His eyes widened, and every nice warm thought he'd been thinking about Tori vanished with a puff from his head.

Right there in bright red lipstick was a message. *C— Remembered something and think we may have found you know what. Gone to check it out. D.J.G. Ciao, T.*

Carter grimaced, rubbing his hands over his face. D.J.G. had to mean Dr. Jim Garvey. Had she come across something to suggest Garvey was their blackmailer? And, if so, what was she checking out? Background information?

A sick feeling rose in the pit of his stomach. With any other agent, he'd assume she'd left the resort and was using the task force resources to run down background on Garvey. But this was Tori he was talking about, and that meant she'd probably gone off on her own to check out the man himself.

Carter sure as hell hoped he was wrong, and as he grabbed his sweatpants and a T-shirt and headed for the door, he said a silent thank-you that he'd been forced to leave his gun with Jonathan. Because if Tori was where he thought she was, he would have been damn sure tempted to use it.

14

NOTHING. Tori slipped out the back door of Dr. Garvey's cabin. Her little adventure hadn't revealed anything, and she was going to have to report to Carter that her gut instinct hadn't panned out.

She stepped from the porch, her mind so preoccupied with running through the clues she didn't even see the man in front of her.

"Tori."

She yelped, and Carter slapped a hand over her mouth, then pulled her into the shadows.

"What the hell are you doing?" he asked, peeling his hand away.

"Me?" she whispered. "You're the one skulking around."

"You're the one breaking into someone's cabin without a search warrant."

"Excuse me?" Tori took a step back. "What the hell are you talking about?"

The anger etched across Carter's face faded, morphing into confusion. "Come with me," he said. He led her in silence to their cabin, settled her on the couch, then started pacing in front of her. Tori stayed quiet throughout the whole process, not sure if she should be amused or irritated.

"Didn't you leave me a note saying you were going to go check out Garvey?"

"Yes, but rather then violate the Fourth Amendment, I thought maybe I'd just try chatting with him." Sarcasm practically dripped from her voice, but she couldn't help it. How dare he think she'd take those kinds of risks?

"You just went to talk with him?"

She nodded.

"Oh." He sat down, looking rather stiff. "About what?"

"About nothing," she said. "I wanted to get a better look at his cabin." The fact was, she'd wanted desperately to rummage through his desk, but she'd stifled the urge.

"Why?"

At the moment, she didn't particularly want to share. But he was her boss, and it was his case, so she leaned against the cushions and started walking him through her thinking. "He needs money," she said. "But he must make a decent living. So I figure he has some big debt that he's trying to cover. Maybe gambling. Maybe the mob. I don't know."

Carter ran his hands through his hair. "How do you know he needs money?"

"He's pawning things," she said. She went on, anticipating his next question. "Jon mentioned that someone from the resort was pawning items. No big deal, right, since they were such small dollars. But it's indicative of a problem, especially if the one doing the pawning is someone who gets paid as much as Garvey."

"But how do you know?"

"I don't for sure. But he collects record albums yet has no stereo. I went to talk to him hoping I'd see a pawn ticket lying around. Better yet, that I'd find a ledger book or something with his debts." She grinned. "Even better, that I'd find drafts of the blackmail letters."

"Did you?"

"Nope. But I'm sure he's the one pawning things. And I just have a feeling he's our blackmailer."

"I don't know, Tori. It seems awfully thin." His cell phone rang, and he flipped it open. "Sinclair." It was Jonathon, and he and Carter had a quick conversation while Tori looked on. When they said goodbye, Carter looked straight at her, respect in his eyes. "You were right."

"I was?"

"Apparently the agent in Houston posing as my father just got a demand for a hundred thou. If he doesn't pay up, the blackmailer's going to go to the press with information about his son's frequent attendance at sordid sex clubs."

"Wow," Tori said, letting the information sink in. She'd been right. She'd trusted her instincts, and she'd been right. Except something about it felt wrong. She couldn't put her finger on it, but something was tickling her brain. Not red flashing neon, but maybe a little pink night-light. Just a tiny warning, and she needed to figure out what it was. She looked at Carter. "What are you going to do?"

"Tomorrow we'll have Jon get a warrant to search Garvey's cabin and office. And I'll have Jon take him in for questioning. That way we won't have to blow our cover."

Tori nodded. Something was still bugging her, but since she couldn't articulate it, she didn't tell Carter. She'd figure it out, though. This had been her case from the get-go, and she didn't intend to falter. She'd told

Carter she was going to solve it—and that was one promise she intended to keep.

"So, IT'S SETTLED then," Carter said, hooking his leg over Jon's desk. "Tomorrow you'll go in for a warrant, and then you'll go out to the resort and bring Garvey in for questioning. Tori and I will maintain our cover for another few days."

Jon nodded. "Gotcha, boss." The phone rang, and Jon scooped it up, turning so he could talk in semiprivacy.

Tori shifted in her chair but didn't say anything. Carter sighed. He still felt like a total heel for assuming she'd gone rushing into Garvey's cabin, gun blazing in one hand and a burning copy of the Constitution in the other. They'd started out at odds, but somewhere along the way they'd really become a team. At least on the job. He was still working on being a team in their personal life.

She'd forgiven him for being a jerk, and for that he was happy. But they were coming to the end of the case, and he'd had no indication that she wanted there to be anything between them after they left the resort. The thought saddened him, but it wasn't something he could focus on right then. They were at a crossroads in the case, and if he wanted his transfer, he needed to bring it in successfully. Once he'd done that, then he could work on convincing Tori that they were right for each other...both undercover and in real life.

Jon hung up the phone and turned, then nodded toward Tori. "You were right about him pawning things. He pawned an antique Victrola and thousands of dollars in jewelry. And after your hunch we did some more digging. Apparently Dr. Garvey does owe a hefty gambling debt.''

"He's our scumbag,'' Carter said. "He's the only one who knows about my sordid sex club addiction, and now we know why he needs the money. After we get Garvey tomorrow, we should be able to wrap this up in a nice little bow for the prosecutors.'' He turned to smile at Tori. "Congratulations, Agent Lowell. You said you'd solve this thing before me, and you did.''

Instead of jumping to the praise in usual Tori fashion, she licked her lips.

"Uh-oh,'' he said. "What's wrong?''

She glanced at him, a grin tugging at her mouth. "I'm that transparent, huh?''

"Pretty much.''

Her head bobbed from side to side, as if she was trying to decide what to say. After a few seconds, she looked from him to Jon and then back. But she still didn't say anything.

"What?'' he asked.

"I was certain Garvey's the guy, but...'' She trailed off, the expression on her face making clear she wasn't giving him the full story.

"But what?''

She shrugged. "But now I'm not so certain.''

Carter ran a hand through his hair. "What? Why not?''

"I...I don't know. I can't put my finger on it.'' She pressed her lips together. "Just call off tomorrow's hounds, okay?''

He shook his head. "Are you kidding? This is our opportunity to wrap things up.''

Once again, she wet her lips with her tongue. "Please, Carter. Trust me.''

"Trust you?" He shoved his hands in his pocket. "You're not trusting me." He thought they'd managed to strike some truce with regard to working together, but apparently he was wrong. "Tell me what you're thinking, Tori. Teamwork, remember. We're partners, and that means we're supposed to trust each other with information. Not keep secrets."

"Carter, please. Just one more day. Why don't *you* trust *my* instincts?"

He set his jaw; he needed to bring this case in, not play guessing games with Tori. "Sorry, agent. We're going in tomorrow. I'm in charge of this mission, and unless you can give me a solid reason not to, we're bringing Garvey in for questioning."

"Fine." She stood up. "You do what you have to do."

With one curt nod to Jon, she turned and headed out of the room. Carter watched her go, not quite sure what had just happened.

"Guess her reputation's well-deserved," Jon said.

Carter looked at him.

"Being unpredictable, I mean. A lone wolf. And competitive as hell."

"Her reputation's made it all the way to a sheriff's department in California?" Even for Tori, that seemed a bit much.

Jon laughed. "No. I did some asking around. I wanted to know about the woman my buddy's falling in love with."

Carter sighed. "Do you think I did the wrong thing?"

"Not from what I've heard. The woman's a wild card, and this assignment means too much to you to screw up."

"It means a lot to Tori, too," Carter said.

"Sure. But considering the competition there was between you two at the academy, she might be trying to sabotage you so she can step in and save the day."

Carter frowned, hating to think that about Tori. Hell, he'd thought that once before—at Quantico—and he'd turned out to be wrong.

But the truth was the truth, and she *was* competitive as hell. And she had told him she'd solve this case.

Still, so much had changed over the last few days. *She'd* changed.

Hadn't she?

Jon shot him a questioning glance. "Unless the rumors about her aren't true. Or unless she's changed." He shrugged. "Only you know the answer to that."

Carter closed his eyes, wishing he did know. He needed to make this mission a success. He couldn't screw it up now, not with so much riding on it. He was falling in love with Tori. But that didn't mean he was sure he could trust her.

After a few minutes, he looked at Jon. "Tomorrow," he said. "Tomorrow you'll bring in Garvey."

THE SUN ROSE over the distant mountains, the light filling the sky as Tori sat on the porch sipping coffee and trying not to cry. She'd done enough crying already, and she hated herself for it. She hadn't cried since her father died, and it pissed her off that she was crying for Carter.

After she'd taken a taxi to the resort, she'd waited for him to come to the cabin, but he never came. She finally checked the voice mail on her cell phone and found his message that he was staying at Jon's so they could work on the game plan for tomorrow.

She made a raw sound in the back of her throat. To think she'd thought she was falling in love with him. She closed her eyes, sighing on an exhale. No, the truth was that she *was* in love with him. But that didn't matter one whit. He didn't trust her. Despite all his talk about being a team, he didn't listen to her. He'd landed the big boss job, and she was just some underling he didn't have to listen to.

Well, fine. Let him ignore her. She'd said she was going to solve this case, and that's what she intended to do.

After he'd called last night, she'd spent the evening going over her notes. She'd been about to doze off when it had hit her—Garvey hadn't seen enough of the victims. There had to be someone working with him. But who?

Then she remembered what Carter said about touch. And how people would open up during moments of intimacy in ways they might not have otherwise done.

That was the connection. She frantically scribbled notes on her charts even as she thought over the details of their time at the resort. It all fit. *Melinda.* Melinda was working with Garvey.

Which meant she'd bolt the second she found out the Feds had taken Garvey in for questioning.

Clearly, Tori had to get her first. For half a second, she considered calling Carter, but she dismissed the idea. He hadn't trusted her enough yesterday to listen to her; there was no reason to believe today would be any different.

Those stupid tears welled again, and she blinked them back. It didn't matter what he thought. All that mattered was that she get her career on the right track. And solving this case would do it for her.

Determined, she stood up. She'd confront the woman herself and, hopefully, get to the bottom of this before Carter and Jon burst in like the cavalry with guns blazing and scared Melinda right off the resort. Tori wouldn't do anything to jeopardize the legality of the mission, of course, but if she could find just a shred of evidence...anything. She needed something to take to Carter so he'd hold off bringing in the rest of the team.

A few minutes later, she climbed the steps to Melinda's porch. After a brief hesitation, she steeled herself as she knocked on the door. Melinda answered, a bathrobe wrapped tight around her.

"Tori, right?" she said. "Class doesn't start for another hour."

"Oh." Tori frowned, not sure where she wanted to go with this. Putting the pieces together after she already had the facts—or ferreting the relevant facts out of a muddled jumble of information—was more her cup of tea than gathering those facts. "I was, uh, hoping to ask you a quick question about massage oils."

That sounded reasonable. Sort of. She hoped it sounded reasonable enough to get her an invitation into Melinda's cabin so she could take a look around.

Melinda smiled. "I've got a few minutes. Shoot."

Tori stood a little straighter, her confidence growing. "Well, Carter and I just finished a session with Dr. Garvey, and he was talking about the power of touch. And so naturally, we wanted to explore that tonight, but I wanted to talk to you about the oils and lotion and stuff. You know, what's the best? Which ones will we enjoy using the most? That kind of thing."

Okay, maybe not the most articulate inquiry, but

she did mention Garvey's name. Maybe she'd get a reaction.

And she did. A slow smile crossed Melinda's face, and her eyes turned dreamy. "Garvey's so great." She pushed open the door and swept her hand over the threshold. "Come on in and I'll see what I've got for you."

Tori followed her through the door, then stopped, not entirely sure why she was hesitating but certain she was uncomfortable going any farther. "You know, maybe I should come back later."

"Really? It's no trouble right now."

"No," Tori said, making up her mind. She'd been the lone wolf too long, trying to follow in her father's footsteps, and she'd never gotten anything but a desk job to show for her trouble. She was good. She was damn good. But that didn't mean she couldn't be better with Carter at her side. Licking her lips, she stood tall, looking Melinda in the eyes. "I think I'll come back with Carter. This is something he and I should do together."

15

CARTER PACED in front of the kitchen window in their cabin, feeling generally like a jerk.

He'd gone on and on to Tori about teamwork, but then he'd struck out when he'd stepped up to the plate. He'd been so damn worried about making a success of the mission he'd forgotten one of the reasons Tori was on the team was that she was an integral part of making it a success. She was smart and she had good instincts. But he'd completely discounted her.

Well, no more.

Resolved, he reached into his pocket and pulled out his cell phone, then called Jon's number.

"Hold off on taking Garvey in," he said as soon as his friend answered.

"Something happen?"

"Today? No. But something happened yesterday that I should have paid attention to."

"Tori."

"She's a good agent. And if she thinks going in would be a mistake, I'm going to listen to her."

"You're the boss," Jon said. "And you know where to find me when you need me."

Carter clicked off and headed into the living room, feeling good about his decision but frustrated since Tori wasn't there to tell it to. Especially since he wanted to ask her if she'd figured out what about the plan to bring Garvey in for questioning was bugging her.

He frowned, wondering where she could be. He looked around the room, an instinctual reaction, since she surely wasn't hiding in the sink or on top of the kitchen table.

But while she might not be, her notes were, and when he saw the papers spread out on the table he wandered over in that direction. Her charts. He picked one up, studying the computer-generated images that had been updated with Tori's boxish handwriting and accented with purple and yellow highlighters.

Intrigued, he picked up the yellow legal pad and started reading through her notes. *Garvey? No intersection. Potpourri. Touch. Melinda?*

She'd circled Melinda's name, punctuating it with an exclamation point in black magic marker. Carter frowned. Apparently Tori thought Melinda was in on the scheme with Garvey. As he flipped through the pages, Carter realized Tori was absolutely right. In every situation where a victim had no connection with Garvey, there was a connection to Melinda. Sighing, he ran his fingers through his hair. They'd never considered the possibility that their blackmailer had a partner. At least, not until Tori considered it.

Once again, he looked around the cabin, wanting to discuss her conclusions and plan their next move. But she wasn't there. He frowned, suddenly certain he knew where she was.

She *could* be at the pool. But knowing Tori the odds were against it.

"Damn it!" He slapped his palm down hard on the table, the sharp sting of pain a counterpoint to the blood boiling in his veins. She was out there; he just knew it. Tori had gone to confront Melinda. She'd completely ignored his role as her superior, she'd completely discounted the possibility of teamwork, and she'd gone out to confront a potential felon without any backup and certainly without a go-ahead.

A frenzy of anger whipped through him, and he stormed out the front door, determined to find Tori and explain to her—in small words if necessary—why she couldn't run off and play Rambo just because she felt like it. "Damn, damn, damn," he muttered, rushing down the stairs and then down the path to the instructors' cabins. Didn't she know how much this assignment meant to him? How the hell could she put it in jeopardy?

But when he reached the turn-off to Melinda's cabin, he stopped. What the hell was he doing? He'd spent the last twenty-four hours suffering under the weight of guilt for not listening to the woman he loved. And now he was assuming that same woman—a woman he knew had brains and talent—was off ruining his case.

Yes, she had a wild streak, and yes, she wanted to succeed, but Tori would never intentionally sabotage a mission. He knew that. No matter how much she wanted to win, he had to trust that she wouldn't hurt the case—or him.

During their academy days, yeah. She would have stabbed him in the back and not even blinked. But she'd changed. He had to believe that. He had to believe it because he loved her. And, most important, he had to believe she loved him right back. Even if she wouldn't admit it.

With regard to their personal relationship, he'd lobbed the ball firmly into her court. With their professional relationship, it was time he did the same thing. He might be her superior in name, but they were a team, and he needed to trust that she knew what she was doing.

He took one last glance down the path toward Melinda's cabin, then headed to his, a little nervous about what Tori was up to, but confident he'd made the right decision.

When he reached his cabin, his faith panned out. Tori was sitting on the porch swing, one foot tucked under her. She lifted her hand in a slight wave. Her sunglasses hid her eyes, but from what he could tell, she didn't look unhappy to see him. Then again, she wasn't jumping for joy. He supposed that was to be expected. He'd been an ass yesterday and, although he'd fixed it, Tori didn't know he'd repented.

"Any minute now, huh?" she asked, looking at her watch.

He frowned. "Pardon?"

She took off her sunglasses. "Any minute now, Jon's going to storm in here and drag Garvey off for questioning."

He hid a smile. "Oh. Right. Well, I doubt Jon ever storms in. And he certainly wouldn't drag Garvey. But it's a moot point since I postponed the operation."

She'd been contemplating her toes peeking out the end of her sandals, but now she looked up, confusion in her eyes. "You what?"

"You were right."

"*I* was right? Me?"

"You."

She pointed to herself. "Me? Tori Lowell? You're saying I was right. You. You're saying that?"

He laughed. "I *was* saying it. I think I'm going to quit now."

Her mouth curved into that perfect smile. "Why?"

"Why am I going to quit saying it? Because you're teasing me."

She scowled at him. "Why am I right?"

"It was too soon. There are other players. Going in after Garvey would've been a mistake." He looked her in the eye. "At the very least, we need to go after Melinda, too."

She pressed her mouth tight, her lips disappearing into one thin line, and he heard her inhale through her nose. "You saw my notes."

"Yup."

She used her toes to push herself on the swing.

"Why didn't you go after her already?" he asked.

She tilted her head to one side. "What makes you think I didn't?"

"You're here, aren't you? And I trust you."

She nodded. "Thank you for that." She took a big breath, then exhaled slowly. "The fact is, I did go. But I couldn't go through with it. I made up an excuse and I left."

Relief flooded his body. He'd had faith in her, and it had paid off.

She looked him in the eye. "It's your call, Sinclair. Tell me how you want to handle it."

"We'll both go. This evening, we'll both go talk to her."

Tori nodded, then her brow creased.

"What?" he asked.

"I just remembered something. The first day we got here. Garvey was in the office—"

"And he said he thought it was more than that," Carter said, his thoughts tracking hers.

"Exactly. He was talking about money."

He nodded. "Garvey thought he owed more than he did." He frowned. "But someone that much in the hole with the Mob should know how much he was in debt for."

"Unless someone else was paying down his debt," Tori said. "Someone who has a crush on him."

"Melinda," Carter said, nodding as the pieces fell into place. "But if Garvey didn't know, then we still have your intersection problem. Not all the victims were Melinda's clients."

"The redhead," Tori said. "Brandi."

Carter held out his hands, clueless.

"She was in the office, remember? Transcribing tapes. Like the kinds of tapes doctors use to dictate their notes. And I saw her and Melinda together."

"So Melinda pumps our redhead and then goes out and works on the victims."

"I'd stake good money on it," Tori said.

"Good. Because we're going to be staking our jobs on it." He looked her in the eye. "I'll tell Jon we're holding off on Garvey indefinitely. In the meantime, I guess we're stuck here at the resort for another few days while we sort through this."

"Yeah?" She stood and walked to him, and his heart picked up its tempo as she rubbed her hand over his chest. "Well, it's a tough job, but somebody's got to do it."

Grinning, he hooked an arm around her waist and pulled her close. "Not bad work, Lowell," he said.

"Not bad, at all." She tilted her head and smiled at him. "You know something, Sinclair? I think we make a pretty good team."

THREE DAYS LATER, Tori stood with Carter in front of the main building and watched as Jon took Melinda away for questioning. A formality, really, since Tori and Carter had spent the last few days putting all the pieces of their theory into place. Bit by bit, they'd confirmed the theory they'd worked through on the porch a few days before.

As the car pulled away, Tori took Carter's hand, a sigh escaping her lips. "I guess this is it," she said.

He nodded. "Tomorrow we go back to the real world. Our real jobs. Whatever they might be."

She nodded. There was an unspoken question in his voice, but she wasn't quite ready to answer him. Wasn't quite ready to admit the truth that was pounding away like a persistent salesman.

"Tori?"

"I..." She looked him in the eyes. "I need to go pack." It was a lame excuse, especially considering he needed to pack, too, and would probably walk along with her to their cabin.

But Carter, bless him, must have heard what she'd really said—*I need some time alone.* He nodded, looking a little sad. "Sure. Go ahead. I need to finish up some paperwork here, anyway."

She whispered a soft thank-you, then turned away and headed down the path toward their cabin, feeling all the more lost because he'd understood her. Her heart swelled, and she bit back tears. More than anyone in her life, Carter understood her. No one else did, no one else really ever had. Not her mom, not Murphy, and certainly not her dad. Hell, her dad hadn't been around enough to really get to know her.

As she reached their cabin, she swallowed a lump of tears in her throat. The truth was, she'd been chasing a dream, and she'd been blaming everybody but herself for never having reached that dream. But Carter was right. She wasn't her dad. She was her own person, and undercover work didn't come easy for her.

She ran her hands through her hair, then sat on the steps, her forehead pressed against her palms. Not only had she blamed other people for her failure, she'd also been chasing the wrong dream. She'd been working toward an illusion, trying to be a superagent, just like her dad, when he really hadn't been so super after all. Oh, sure, he'd loved her and her mom. She'd never doubt that. But he'd never really been there for them. Was he really someone she wanted to emulate? Especially when following in her father's footsteps meant turning away from the one thing in her life that really meant something? That really made her happy?

Carter.

Carter understood her. She smiled. Hell, Carter put up with her. And there weren't many men out there who fit that bill. But Carter did, and it was time she told him.

Gathering her resolve, she stood, wanting to go find him. But he was right there—walking down the path toward her. She flashed him a watery smile. She should have known he'd be there for her.

"Hey," he said, his hands shoved in his pockets. "I know you wanted to be alone, but I—"

"No." She held out her hand for him. "I'm glad you're here. There's something I want to tell you."

"Good," he said. "Because there's something I want to tell you, too." He took a deep breath. "I want you, Tori. I know I've said it before, but I really want you to listen to me this time. I want to make this work. I think we can do it."

"But—"

"I know. You want an undercover assignment. But we can make it work. People have." He took her hands. "*We* can."

She fought more tears, only this time tears of joy. "No, Carter. I'm not—"

"Don't push me away," he said, "because I'm not taking no for an answer. We're perfect for each other." He grinned, his eyes dancing. "And, besides, who else would put up with you?"

A tear escaped, cutting a path down her cheek, and she laughed in spite of herself. "No one. You're it, I'm afraid."

"I want you," he said. "I want *us*."

"Thank you," she whispered. She wrapped her arms around him and rested her head on his shoulder.

He stroked her hair. "You've worked hard. You deserve an undercover assignment," Carter said.

She took a deep breath, then pulled back, looking him in the eye. "I'm telling Murphy I want to stay in analysis."

Carter's throat moved as he swallowed. "What?"

"I don't want an undercover assignment, after all," she said.

"But why?"

She took a deep breath, knowing that he of all people would understand. "I've been following a borrowed dream," she finally said. "I'm not my dad." She shrugged. "I spent years wishing for the wrong thing, and you know how much I hate being wrong."

He stroked her hair. "Are you sure?"

She licked her lips, hating to say the rest but knowing she had to because it was true. "I'm sure. The truth is, I'm not very good at undercover work." She snuggled closer. "I guess I was wrong about that, too."

"You're fine at it," Carter said. "You solved this case."

"We solved this case." She kissed his cheek, feeling warm all over simply from his unhesitating support. "It's okay," she said. "Just because I'm not the best undercover agent on the planet doesn't mean my ego's going to shrivel up and die." She looked him in the eye. "Not anymore."

"So what do you want?"

"Analysis. I'm good at it and I like it. I've always liked it. I just let myself believe I should be doing something else."

"Just like Dorothy," he said.

She squinted, shaking her head. "Who?"

"You know, Dorothy. There's no place like home. You went looking for something better, and what you wanted was right under your nose."

She stroked his cheek. "Yeah. That's exactly it. Right under my nose." She ran her teeth across her lower lip. "There's something else, too," she said. She swallowed. She loved him. There was no doubt in her mind. But she'd never told anyone that before, and it was hard. Especially since she didn't know how Carter would react. He'd said he wanted them to see how their relationship developed, but what did that mean, really? He'd never told her he loved her. And if he didn't... If she lost the bet she was making on her heart...

He took her hand. "What?"

"I love you," she said, blurting the words out before she talked herself out of it.

A wide grin split his face. "I was hoping you were

going to say that," he said. He tugged her into his embrace, then kissed the top of her head. "I love you, too."

She sagged against him, relief and happiness flooding her body.

His fingers stroked her back, the gesture both reassuring and enticing. "I love you more than anything."

She leaned back, grinning at him. "Not more than I love you."

He stroked her cheek. "You know what, sweetheart? On this, I'm happy to let you win."

_____Epilogue_____

THE STEADY BUZZ of the alarm clock woke Tori. She peeled open her eyes and gave it a dirty look, not because of the noise, but because she was going to have to scoot out of Carter's arms if she wanted to turn the darn thing off.

Trying to ignore it, she snuggled closer, wondering how her husband was sleeping through that ruckus. Grinning, she repeated the word in her mind—_husband_. They'd been married a full year, and the word still gave her chills.

Carter was hers, and she was Carter's.

"Make it stop," he mumbled, pulling the pillow over his head.

She rolled over and hit the control button, then scooted over and pried the pillow off his face. "Time to wake up," she said, inching the sheet down and dropping kisses on his chin, his neck, his chest. "Unless you want me to just keep going...." She kept her voice low, seductive, and lifted her head only slightly to catch his reaction.

"That plan has a definite appeal," he said, stroking her hair. "But we told Phyllis last night we'd be down for breakfast."

"It's our anniversary," she said. "Phyllis will understand." For that matter, Tori was pretty sure the motherly B and B owner was just as excited about the occasion as Tori and Carter were.

"And Jonathon's dropping by later to say hello."

Tori groaned. "Okay, okay. I'll put on clothes." She rolled out of bed, pretending to be annoyed. Actually, she was looking forward to seeing Jonathon. Since Melinda had accepted a plea bargain and gone off to prison, there hadn't been a need for Tori or Carter to spend time in Santa Barbara preparing for trial. And the Texas field office where she and Carter were assigned wasn't exactly close to Jonathon's Santa Barbara sheriff's department.

She pulled a bathing suit out of the top drawer. "What do you think? Time for a swim before breakfast?"

He propped himself up in bed, a wolfish grin on his face. "Sweetheart, if you wear that we won't get to breakfast."

"Beach. Swimming. Vacation. Remember?"

He patted the bed. "Naked. Sex. Anniversary. Remember?"

Tori laughed. "You had your chance, mister, and you said no. I want to swim out to that buoy and back."

"So much for relaxing," he said, slipping out of bed. He grabbed a pair of swim trunks from the suitcase on the floor and pulled them on.

Tori watched the view with longing. Maybe staying in bed all day wasn't such a bad idea. But no...places to go and people to see.

"Okay," he said. "I'm ready."

He grabbed a couple of towels while she put on her suit, then they headed down, promising Phyllis they'd be right back.

"No more than half an hour," Carter said.

"Half an hour?" Tori asked as they crossed the beach. She took his hand in hers. "I can make it there and back in fifteen at the most."

"Is that a challenge, agent?" Carter asked.

"Me? Compete with you?" She pressed a hand to her chest. "I'm shocked."

As Carter laughed, she cocked her head toward the water. "Last one to the water is a rotten egg," she said. And with that, she took off running, Carter right at her heels.

**Receive 2 FREE Trade books with 4 proofs
of purchase from Harlequin Temptation® books.**

HARLEQUIN®
Temptation.

You will receive:

Dangerous Desires: Three complete novels by
Jayne Ann Krentz, Barbara Delinsky and Anne Stuart

and

Legacies of Love: Three complete novels by
Jayne Ann Krentz, Stella Cameron and Heather Graham

**Simply complete the order form and mail to:
"Temptation 2 Free Trades Offer"**

In U.S.A.	In CANADA
P.O. Box 9057	P.O. Box 622
3010 Walden Avenue	Fort Erie, Ontario
Buffalo, NY 14269-9057	L2A 5X3

YES! Please send me *Dangerous Desires* and *Legacies of Love,* without
cost or obligation except shipping and handling. Enclosed are 4 proofs
of purchase from September or October 2002 Harlequin Temptation
books and $3.75 shipping and handling fees. New York State residents
must add applicable sales tax to shipping and handling charge.
Canadian residents must add 7% GST to shipping and handling charge.

Name (PLEASE PRINT)

Address   Apt. #

City   State/Prov.   Zip/Postal Code

TEMPTATION 2 FREE TRADES OFFER TERMS
To receive your FREE trade books, please complete the above
form. Mail it to us with 4 proofs of purchase, one of which can
be found in the lower right-hand corner of this page. Requests
must be received no later than November 30, 2002. Please
include $3.75 for shipping and handling fees and applicable
taxes as stated above. The 2 FREE Trade books are valued at
$12.95 U.S./$14.95 CAN. each. All orders are subject to
approval. Terms and prices are subject to change without
notice. Please allow 6-8 weeks for delivery. Offer good in
Canada and the U.S. only. Offer good while quantities last.
Offer limited to one per household.

Temptation.

2 **FREE TRADES OFFER**
One Proof of Purchase

HARLEQUIN®
Makes any time special ®

HTPOPFT

More fabulous reading from
the Queen of Sizzle!

LORI
FOSTER

with

Forever and Always

Back by popular demand are the scintillating stories of
Gabe and Jordan Buckhorn. They're gorgeous, sexy
and single…at least for now!

Available wherever books are sold—September 2002.

And look for Lori's **brand-new** single title,
CASEY in early 2003

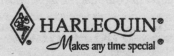

If you enjoyed what you just read,
then we've got an offer you can't resist!

Take 2 bestselling love stories FREE!

Plus get a FREE surprise gift!

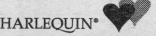

Princes...Princesses...
London Castles...New York Mansions...
To live the life of a royal!

In 2002, Harlequin Books lets you escape to a world of royalty with these royally themed titles:

Temptation:
January 2002—*A Prince of a Guy* (#861)
February 2002—*A Noble Pursuit* (#865)

American Romance:
The Carradignes: American Royalty (Editorially linked series)
March 2002—*The Improperly Pregnant Princess* (#913)
April 2002—*The Unlawfully Wedded Princess* (#917)
May 2002—*The Simply Scandalous Princess* (#921)
November 2002—*The Inconveniently Engaged Prince* (#945)

Intrigue:
The Carradignes: A Royal Mystery (Editorially linked series)
June 2002—*The Duke's Covert Mission* (#666)

Chicago Confidential
September 2002—*Prince Under Cover* (#678)

The Crown Affair
October 2002—*Royal Target* (#682)
November 2002—*Royal Ransom* (#686)
December 2002—*Royal Pursuit* (#690)

Harlequin Romance:
June 2002—*His Majesty's Marriage* (#3703)
July 2002—*The Prince's Proposal* (#3709)

Harlequin Presents:
August 2002—*Society Weddings* (#2268)
September 2002—*The Prince's Pleasure* (#2274)

Duets:
September 2002—*Once Upon a Tiara/Henry Ever After* (#83)
October 2002—*Natalia's Story/Andrea's Story* (#85)

Celebrate a year of royalty with Harlequin Books!

Available at your favorite retail outlet.

HARLEQUIN®
Makes any time special ®